SHADOWS OF SERENITY

A HARRY SINCLAIR COZY TRAVEL MYSTERY

BOOK 1

SABINA O.

CORTIJO BERRUGUILLA

For permission requests, write to:

Sabina Ostrowska, penname Sabina O.

textworkshop.org

sabina.a.ostrowska@gmail.com

First Edition

ISBN: 978-84-09-62088-3 (paperback edition)

ASIN: B0CSDHTBXN (e-book edition)

WHAT READERS SAY ABOUT THIS BOOK

"I loved the exotic setting of Koh Samui, and thought the author did a lovely job depicting culture and surroundings. The mystery was so intriguing I could never stop at "just one more chapter", and many of the lies and clues that were revealed shocked me."

"The traveler in me enjoyed the exotic food recipes and the way the atmosphere was described. Sabina's writing is great. The way she writes made the book feel calm while also building up the mystery towards the end. I'm a sucker for mystery, and this didn't disappoint. I can't wait to read what comes next!"

"I started reading this novel 2 days ago with a "Sound of the sea" background. The descriptions of the setting of the story, the characters, and the day to day life on the retreat made me feel like i was there and part of the group. The suspense stayed whole up to the big reveal and I actually feel disappointed with myself for not having guessed who the culprit was..."

"I read this book sitting by the pool in Spain, and it really transported me to Thailand. I didn't guess who it was until it was revealed but suspected several others. Great story and good characters."

SABINA O.

A Harry Sinclair Cozy Travel Mystery series so far:

Shadows of Serenity

Moonlit Secrets

Whispers of Lotus Villa (1st June 2025)

Sabina's Humorous Non-fiction Series:

The Crinkle Crankle Wall: Our First Year in Andalusia

A Hoopoe on the Nispero Tree: Our Andalusian Adventure Continues

Olive Leaf Tea: Time to Settle

CONTENTS

PROLOGUE

The sun began its slow descent, casting a warm golden glow over the coconut plantation on the idyllic shore of Koh Samui. A middle-aged man with a sun-kissed complexion walked away from the beach, his bare feet sinking into the powdery sand. The rhythmic rustling of swaying coconut palms provided a soothing backdrop to this tropical paradise.

As he took a shortcut across the plantation to his hut, the restless canopy of palm fronds overhead created a mesmerizing dance of light and shadow. The air carried the faint scent of coconut mingled with the ocean breeze. The verdant surroundings embraced him, momentarily allowing him to forget the worries of his everyday life.

With the retreat's buildings in sight, he was confronted with the intoxicating scent of a frangipani bush he passed by. Lost in the stillness of his surroundings, his serenity was abruptly shattered by a strange sound emanating from behind. Instinctively, he turned, his eyes widening in recognition. Before he could defend himself, the back of his head was met with a sharp impact.

Collapsing to the ground, and with his senses fading, he painfully rolled onto his back, and his gaze settled on the familiar face standing above him.

"You won't hurt anyone else," the voice whispered, a heavy hammer in the killer's hand, ready to administer the final blow.

Realization struck him like a lightning bolt, fear mingling with his final breath. He should have recognized his killer earlier. They had met before.

As his life force slowly ebbed away, his vision blurred, but the vibrant green, red, and yellow hues of the tropical landscape flashed in random sequences across his dwindling consciousness. The palms stood tall and proud, their slender trunks adorned with clusters of ripe coconuts, and the surrounding foliage contrasted with the azure expanse of the nearby ocean, creating a picture-perfect scene that betrayed the darkness lurking within.

When his last breath escaped his lips, the truth he carried within him slipped away into the shadows.

CHAPTER 1

TWO DAYS EARLIER

Harry sat cross-legged on the sandy beach, her steady gaze fixed on the shimmering turquoise waters of Koh Samui Bay. The rhythmic lapping of the gentle waves against the shore created a soothing melody, inviting her to dive deep into her thoughts. With her laptop perched across her bare legs, she again attempted to add a paragraph to her travel blog, but her thoughts meandered away, irresistibly pulled by the currents of memories and past regrets.

She closed her eyes, feeling the warmth of the tropical sun on her skin, and allowed her mind to wander back to her former life in the bustling streets of New York City, evoking the sights, sounds, and scents of a place that had once consumed her every waking moment. The constant hustle and bustle, the deafening cacophony of horns and sirens, and the polluted air that choked the city.

Her mind drifted to her tiny studio apartment, where she had spent countless hours hunched over a cheap wooden desk, her world confined to the space between four walls built far too close to each other. She had been subject to a whirlwind of deadlines and demanding editors; their pressure mounting with each passing day. Her big lifestyle magazine job had seemed glamorous at first, but it had slowly eroded her spirit, suffocating her love for writing. The Editor-in-Chief felt that Harry had a real talent for bringing the homes of the rich New Yorkers to life and delegated to her the writing of cookie-cutter pieces in which famous women showcased their city dwellings.

"So glad I studied Whitman and Dickinson so that I can write about the Kardashians' walk-in closets," she would joke to her friends in private.

One morning on the C train on her way to an editorial meeting, Harry had watched a young man board with a female pit bull on a short lead in one hand and a paint bucket and brushes in the other. Although people greeted the dog, they ignored each other, and a middle-aged woman fell asleep over her Kindle even though it was just nine a.m. Everyone around seemed hopelessly tired and hollow. At the next stop, the pit bull and its owner left the train, and a candy salesman boarded. He announced his presence to the disinterested crowd. The man was from Colombia and had just arrived in the city. He couldn't find work, so he sold candy in hopes of getting a few dollars to get by. As he walked along the train, people looked away.

The man had undertaken a perilous journey across a continent to fulfill his dream, and here he was selling candy, Harry thought to herself. She wished she had some cash to buy candy, but she used her cell phone to pay for things in the city and never carried any cash. For the rest of the day, Harry could not stop thinking of the man's life. *He's being ignored and struggles every day, yet he perseveres. It would seem I am merely leading a life of quiet desperation.* A longing for freedom had seized her soul that day. A desire to break free from the constraints of her life, to seek new horizons, and to regain the joy of storytelling.

"What's the worst that could happen?" she said, explaining her decision to a friend over drinks. "I can't go on like this, and with my fibromyalgia, sitting for hours in front of a laptop is excruciating. I need to be out there, sucking out the marrow of life."

And so, she made the bold decision to 'leave it all behind her' to embark on a journey that would take her around the world, documenting her adventures on her travel blog.

As Harry opened her eyes and escaped the stressful memory of her life in New York City, the serene panorama of Koh Samui greeted her. The contrast between her past life and the present moment couldn't have been starker. Here, the air was clean and fragrant with the sweet scent of tropical flowers. The spacious expanse of the beach beckoned her to explore; to embrace the freedom she had yearned for.

She shifted her gaze from her laptop to the breathtaking bay, its crystal-clear water inviting her to plunge in. The vibrant hues of the sky and the sea merged seamlessly, forming a breathtaking spectacle that mirrored the transformation she had undergone since leaving her old life behind.

Just as she finished reminiscing about the journey that had brought her here, a gentle electronic ping interrupting her thoughts. Her phone displayed a reminder: "Yoga session – 6:00 PM." With a satisfied smile, she closed her laptop, slipped it into her satchel, and rose from the sandy embrace of the beach. She reminded herself of the need to live for the present moment while continuing with the task of weaving her story, one adventure at a time.

With a renewed sense of purpose, Harry left the beach behind, ready to immerse herself into the calming practice of yoga, finding balance and tranquility in this corner of the world that had become her haven. As she walked away, she couldn't help but feel immensely grateful for the serendipitous twists and turns of Fate that had led her to this wonderful place where the turquoise bay held the promise of endless possibilities. Had it not been for her fibromyalgia diagnosis, she would be currently walking across a filthy metro station to catch the C train and not across a pristine beach to a yoga session. While many people in her support group in New York focused on the daily pains caused by the condition and devoted the sessions to fishing for pity, Harry saw her illness as a call to action. A cliché warning not to waste the precious time we have. Instead of feeling sorry for herself, Harry felt grateful that she could walk the Earth and explore its natural beauty, share laughs with friends, and make plans for the future.

As Harry approached the pavilion, she noticed a couple already waiting outside. The man stood tall, his salt-and-pepper hair reflecting the sunlight, while his wife fidgeted nervously beside him. The husband seemed to be going through a midlife crisis, evidenced by a shiny silver earring; a hint of rebellion against the passage of time. The wife, on the other hand, appeared slightly overweight and carried an air of self-consciousness, her eyes darting around as if searching for reassurance. Both were dressed in similar harem pants and loose cotton shirts with colorful patterns of elephants and mandalas.

With a warm smile, Harry approached them. "Hello there! Are you here for the yoga session?"

The woman nodded. "Yes, we just arrived today."

"I'm Harry. Welcome to the retreat."

"Pleasure to meet you, Harry. I'm James, and this is my wife, Lisa. We're so excited to be here. The place is beautiful."

"Yes, even better than the photos," Lisa said, speaking softly.

The trio engaged in light conversation as they awaited the start of the yoga session.

"Hello, hello!" a cheerful voice interrupted them.

It was Mary—a middle-aged woman from Nebraska known for her almost uncontrollable chattiness. Harry introduced the newcomers, and Mary continued to talk to them as if they were good friends, somewhat oblivious that the places and people she was referring to were completely unknown to the couple.

"We were in the Lime Tree, and Anthony ordered grilled crab, but you won't believe it! They served him the whole crab in a shell. It took him an hour to pull out the tiny morsels of meat! He was not happy about it."

"Lime Tree is a very nice restaurant near the retreat, and Anthony is one of the guests here," Harry explained to the confused couple. "He's over there."

Harry waved at an elderly gentleman in white linen pants and a beautifully embroidered Indian-style shirt. He waved back at her but sat down on his mat and closed his eyes, signaling that he wanted to be left alone. *An afternoon with Mary would do it to anyone*, Harry thought. While Harry appreciated Mary's friendly nature, her mind often drifted away while Mary went on.

As Harry set up her yoga mat, she waved at the other guests getting ready for the session. People were chatting about their experiences at the retreat so far, sharing stories of early morning beach walks, relaxing spa treatments, and the calming effect of the island's natural beauty. Harry had only been at the retreat for a few days and could recognize some faces, but she hadn't made any friends. She couldn't help but notice that Lisa looked out of place in this tranquil paradise, as if she were an observer, not a willing participant.

James, on the other hand, was eager to fit in and explore the island. His eyes lit up as Mary described some boats trips that she had taken—the hidden coves, spectacular coral reefs, and emerald lagoons. He explained that he had seen them in photos on the internet and could not wait to experience them in real life. Harry, an avid explorer herself, listened intently, feeling a kinship with James's enthusiasm for adventure. She was about to ask if they wanted to go with her on a boat trip organized by the retreat, when Yvonne, the yoga instructor, appeared. Wearing large hoop earrings adorned with long feathers that danced in the gentle breeze, she resembled an ethereal being. Her short gray hair framed her symmetrical face, accentuating her set-back shoulders and strong, athletic physique. As she spoke, her voice carried a sense of calm and wisdom, instantly captivating those around her.

"*Namaste*, and welcome, everyone. As we gather here today amidst the serenity of nature, let us take a moment to honor the journey that has brought us together. In the next hour, I invite you to embark on a voyage within, exploring the depths of your own mindfulness and tranquility. Let this session be a sanctuary for your mind, body, and spirit—a space where you can release, relax, and reconnect with your inner self. Remember, there is no 'right' or 'wrong' here, only the path to greater self-awareness and peace. So, let's breathe together, move together, and awaken the harmony that resides within us all. Welcome to this moment of stillness in our beautiful retreat. Let's begin."

Everyone fell into a comfortable silence and settled on their respective mats ready to follow the instructor's directions. The session began with breathing exercises, and then Yvonne guided them through a series of stretches and poses, allowing their minds to find peace in a world that is often without peace. Harry often wondered how quickly the time passed during the sessions, as she immersed herself in the here and now. Concentrating on the seashell wind chimes decorating the open-air pavilion, and listening to the sea, she felt invincible. Soon the session was over, and Yvonne was sharing some announcements of the next day's activities at the retreat.

With a final exhale, Harry, James, and Lisa exchanged smiles, signaling a sense of camaraderie.

"Would you like to come over for a drink and some light supper?" Lisa asked Harry as they gathered their belongings. "We have a nice Chardonnay chilling in the fridge, and we're going to order sushi from a nearby restaurant."

"Wine and sushi? My two favorite things!" Harry said enthusiastically, trying not to reveal how surprised she was that the invitation came from Lisa.

I'm a terrible judge of character. Harry thought to herself as they agreed on the time and Lisa explained which hut was theirs. *Perhaps Lisa is just jet-lagged and tired; that's why she came off as standoffish. You really shouldn't judge a book by its cover.*

Talking to herself was a habit that Harry had acquired when she moved to New York. As a writer, she would often spend days on her own in her studio. New York was a very different place from the small town she grew up in with her grandparents. There, you could not get away from people, even though the total population was only a few thousand. In the city, people didn't speak to you unless they had to. To help with the loneliness, Harry often spoke to herself, discussing her work and debating what to order for supper. She would have liked to adopt a rescue dog or a cat, but her landlord did not allow pets, and she hadn't been sure where her life was heading.

Back in her hut, Harry dropped off her satchel on the bed, showered, and changed from her yoga outfit into shorts and a T-shirt. She walked through the resort's winding paths until she reached Lisa and James's hut nestled amidst the tropical foliage. Lisa and James were already on the porch, drinking wine in the soft ambiance of the lanterns. They hadn't changed since they came from the session, which suggested they may have already had a drink or two

"Welcome to our humble abode," James said, greeting her jovially. "One glass of Chardonnay coming up." He disappeared inside the hut.

Harry made herself comfortable on one of the porch's chairs.

"It's so serene here," Lisa said blissfully.

Harry had to agree as she marveled at the moonlit scene spread out before them, the moon's silver rays shimmering upon the tranquil bay. A gentle breeze carried the salty scent of the sea, enticing her senses. Soon, James was back on the porch with Harry's wine, and the small party clinked their glasses and enjoyed the moment and each other's company.

As they indulged in the expertly prepared sushi that had been delivered to their porch, Lisa opened up about her struggle with her weight. "A friend of mine recommended this yoga retreat to help me shed some pounds," she admitted with a sigh. "But to be honest, the food in Thailand has been so good, and the wine so cheap, I don't see how I'm going to lose any weight here.

"I know what you mean," Harry said, hoping Lisa wouldn't dwell on the topic for too long. She was not a fan of oversharing and found it uncomfortable when strangers did it. But Lisa was in need of a sympathetic ear and kept talking about her personal struggles.

"When the kids were younger, I was always so busy, you know? There were never enough hours in a day, but ever since the kids left for college, I've found myself alone at home with not much to do. I'd watch TV and eat. It's been difficult to find a new purpose in life."

Harry listened attentively, offering a supportive smile. "It can be challenging when life goes through such transitions. But you're here now, making steps toward finding a balance between life and taking care of yourself."

Before Lisa could respond, James interjected, his eyes lighting up with enthusiasm. "Speaking of taking care of ourselves, you should see my motorboat," he exclaimed. "It's a classic, a true piece of craftsmanship. The woodwork inside and out is amazing. I'd been dreaming of buying it for a long time, and now that the kids are on their own, I decided to do it. It's my favorite place in the world, being at sea, feeling the wind against my face. Boats give me a real sense of freedom."

Lisa rolled her eyes playfully, the hint of a smile tugging at the corners of her lips. "Yes, James, we've heard all about your motorboat," she teased. "But let's not forget, we're here to unwind and let go of our worries, at least for a little while."

Harry chuckled, enjoying the light banter between the couple. It was evident that James sought adventure and wanted to relive his youthful years at this midlife crossroads. Lisa, on the other hand, craved self-acceptance and a renewed sense of purpose.

As they shared stories and laughter under the moonlit sky, the evening unfolded with a comforting ease. The sounds of the ocean waves and the delicate clinking of glasses accompanied the warmth of new friendship. Harry, James, and Lisa gazed out across the moonlit bay and a fleeting moment of kinship was forged through shared vulnerabilities and the search for purpose amidst the ebb and flow of life.

As Lisa and Harry engaged in a heartfelt conversation, Lisa reached for her cell phone and began flipping through a series of cherished photos, her eyes brimming with pride and affection. She handed the phone to Harry, offering her a glimpse into her world.

"These are my children," Lisa beamed, pointing to an image showing a handsome young man and a vibrant young woman. "This is Chris, my older son. He's studying to be a medical doctor. Such a bright future ahead of him. And this is Clara, my younger daughter. She's studying history online while working part-time at a small museum in Chicago. Both of them are my pride and joy."

Harry's eyes sparkled as she observed the genuine delight and love emanating from Lisa and James. It was evident that their children held a special place in their hearts, their accomplishments standing as a testament to the nurture and support they had received.

Demonstrating an eagerness to continue the conversation, James turned his attention to Harry. "So, Harry, where are you from?" he inquired, a genuine curiosity shining through his friendly gaze.

Harry paused for a moment, her expression flickering with a hint of introspection. "I'm originally from a small town in New York State. Ithaca? You've probably never heard of it," she replied with a touch of nostalgia. "I loved Ithaca, but it's so small. Everyone in your life, including your teachers, shop assistants, bankers, and accountants, knows each other and is in everyone's business. I love it. But I've always had a restless spirit and the desire to explore beyond the familiar. I couldn't imagine myself living there for the rest of my life. That's why I went to Columbia University and then stayed in New York, working for a lifestyle magazine and freelancing for other news outlets."

Lisa leaned forward, her eyes filled with warmth. "Your parents must be so proud of you traveling around the world and supporting yourself by doing what you love," she said, with admiration in her voice.

A subtle change swept across Harry's face, a fleeting glimpse of a deeper story yet untold. She hesitated for a moment, her gaze drifting toward the moonlit bay. "Well, my parents passed away when I was a child," she responded, her voice tinged with sadness. "I grew up with my grandparents who, as you say, are so proud of me and support everything I decide to do."

Lisa's expression softened, understanding the unspoken depth of Harry's words. Sensing Harry's hesitance, she chose not to pry further, allowing the silence to settle between them like a familiar embrace.

The atmosphere was now marred by a mixture of emotions—sadness, longing, and unspoken desires. Each individual carried their own burdens and triumphs, their own tales woven into the tapestry of their lives. Harry, with her yearning for freedom and self-expression, found solace in the company of James and Lisa. Tonight's conversation had become a refuge from her past.

As the conversation continued to flow, the glasses of wine were refilled, and a light-hearted gossip session began between Harry, Lisa, and James. They leaned in closer together, their voices lowered in conspiratorial tones.

"What do you think of Yvonne, the yoga instructor?" Lisa asked, a mischievous glimmer in her eyes.

Harry nodded, a smile playing on her lips. "Oh, Yvonne. She's quite the character, isn't she? I had the chance to chat with her when I arrived. She's the co-owner of the retreat. She's been here on Koh Samui for a while now."

Lisa leaned in yet further, her curiosity piqued. "Tell us more," she urged.

"Well," Harry began, "Yvonne moved to Koh Samui after she retired from working on cruise ships. With her savings, she bought this piece of land, and she started off by renting a few huts on the beach to backpackers. But over the last decade, she has managed to transform it into this beautiful yoga retreat we're all enjoying now."

"Yvonne's quite an interesting woman. A true free spirit, you could say," Lisa chimed in, adding her own insight.

Harry nodded in agreement. "Absolutely. She's originally from the Netherlands and has brought Dutch business savvy to the island. It's clear she's passionate about yoga and creating a space for others to find inner peace."

"And I've heard her wife, Marieke, is more business-oriented. A perfect balance, I suppose," James added.

"Exactly. As I understand it, Marieke runs the hotel side of things, taking care of the business aspects and attending to guests from all over the world, while Yvonne brings her creativity and love for yoga to the forefront. Together, they've built something truly remarkable."

The three shared a moment of reflection, contemplating the dynamics of Yvonne and Marieke's partnership. It was evident that their complementary strengths had played a significant role in the success of the yoga retreat.

It was late into the night when Harry left. The moon cast its soft glow upon James and Lisa, and the night air grew cooler. Before they turned in, Lisa looked at her husband and asked.

"So, what do you think?"

"I think she's perfect for the job. Has a good reason to travel around and seems gullible enough."

"I agree, but we need a few more like her."

"It won't be a problem finding them here among all the hipster backpackers. Let's keep our eyes open."

Chapter 2

A New Guest

The dawn sun cast a warm glow over the beach as the participants of the early mindfulness session gathered and waited for Yvonne to begin. Harry found a comfortable spot on the soft sand and closed her eyes. She breathed in the smell of the ocean and touched the wet sand. Exhaling, she then took three more deep breaths. She felt embraced by nature. Soon, she heard Yvonne's soft voice.

"Good morning, everyone," Yvonne said, her voice soothing yet filled with vitality. "Before we begin, I'd like to introduce our newest guest, Amaya, who arrived last night and really wanted to join us early this morning."

"Hello, everyone!" A young woman in her mid-to-late twenties waved shyly as she flattened the sand to put her mat on it.

Her dark, curly hair bounced with each nod of her head, and her lively smile revealed a pair of charming dimples. Amaya had a calm but confident presence, and Harry felt she might be a kindred spirit.

"Let's begin by finding a comfortable position, either seated or lying down," Yvonne said, her voice interrupted Harry's musings. "Where you can feel at ease yet fully present.

Close your eyes if that is comfortable for you, and allow yourself to arrive fully in this moment."

Throughout the mindfulness session, Harry's thoughts intermittently wandered from the present to her childhood. At first, she felt content with herself—the warm feeling of being loved washing over her body. It brought back a cherished memory of sitting on a worn-out sofa next to her Grandad, watching *Jeopardy!* with him while Grandma prepared their dinner in the open-plan kitchen. She and Grandad would shout out the answers, competing to be first. Harry inhaled, and the smell of her grandparents' living room and kitchen came to life. But then, an unwanted thought occurred to her—the reason why she had lived with her grandparents and not in her own house. She took a deep breath and put that thought away.

She opened her eyes, trying to focus on the present moment, allowing the sounds of the crashing waves and Yvonne's gentle words to come to the fore. The rhythmic rise and fall of her breath helped to ground her, providing refuge amidst the swirl of emotions that clouded her thoughts.

As the session concluded, Harry's eyes met Amaya's gaze. Determined to make a new friend, Harry approached.

"Hi there, I'm Harry," she said, extending a hand in greeting.

"Nice to meet you, Harry. I'm Amaya," she replied, her voice carrying a hint of California's laid-back charm. "That's a unique name for a girl. Is it short for Henrietta?"

"You guessed it! Henrietta Sinclair, at your service!" Harry chuckled. "I don't know what my parents were thinking—sounds very distinguished, like an old suffragette or an heiress. If I had been a boy, I would've been named Atticus—after my mom's favorite book character. So, I'm glad it turned out differently," she confessed with a sigh of relief.

Amaya nodded, a shared understanding evident in her gaze. "You've had a narrow escape. Atticus Sinclair! Kids at school would have been merciless."

They both laughed.

"I love your pink hair. It suits you."

"Thank you." Harry grabbed a loose strand of her light pink hair and looked at it appraisingly. "Do you think so? I had it done last week but haven't decided yet if I want to keep it that way."

"You definitely should."

"I was planning to rent a scooter this morning and go for a ride around the island," Harry said, introducing her idea. "I was wondering if you'd like to join me. I've spoken to some other guests, and they told me it's an amazing ride. The trip itself takes an hour or so, but we could stop for snacks or a swim."

"Actually, that would be wonderful, and a great way for me to explore the island on my first day."

"Perfect. Shall we meet outside the reception after breakfast? I'll ask Marieke to prepare two scooters for us."

"That sounds great. I'll see you then."

The morning sun cast a golden hue over Koh Samui as Harry and Amaya geared up for their scooter tour around the island. The air was filled with the salty tang of the sea, mingled with the sweet fragrance of frangipani flowers. They picked up their scooters from Nop, one of the workers at the retreat. Nop, who often took the guests on tours around the island, gave them a quick briefing on the scooters and a map marked with must-see spots.

"Ready for this?" Harry asked, adjusting her helmet and sunglasses, her excitement palpable.

"Born ready," Amaya replied with a grin.

They kicked off, blending into the flow of island traffic. The road took them past bustling markets filled with the vibrant colors of tropical fruits and the lively chatter of locals bargaining. They continued on, the landscape transforming as they left the town's hustle and bustle behind.

"That's amazing!" Harry called out over the hum of the scooter engines, pulling over at a viewpoint overlooking the azure waters of the Gulf of Thailand. The sea stretched out to the horizon, dotted with the silhouettes of distant islands.

Amaya parked her scooter next to Harry's and removed her helmet to better take in the breathtaking panorama. "It's like something off a postcard," she marveled, her eyes reflecting the deep blues of the sea.

They snapped a few photos, the moment immortalized against the backdrop of endless water and sky. Back on the road, they followed the coastal path, the sea a constant companion on their right. Palm trees swayed in the gentle breeze, their leaves rustling like whispers of the island's secrets.

As they approached a secluded beach, Harry suggested a break. "How about a swim?" she proposed, pointing to a narrow track leading down to the shore.

"Perfect timing. I was starting to feel the heat," Amaya agreed, following Harry down the path. The beach was a slice of paradise, with powdery white sand and crystal-clear waters. They spent some time playing in the waves, the cool water a refreshing respite from the tropical heat.

Afterward, while drying off under the sun, Amaya said, "I could stay on this island forever, but I have to be in Bangkok in a couple of weeks."

"What do you do?"

"It's complicated," Amaya's eyes scanned the horizon as she spoke. "I studied accounting, and I got a cushy job in a bank soon after I graduated, but things did not go according to my plan. Like so many others, I lost my job during the pandemic. It was a wake-up call; a chance to reevaluate my priorities in life. I was very depressed after I lost my job—I spent days sitting on my sofa staring at my phone. Nobody was hiring. That's when I saw an article online about a retired widow who had been traveling the world looking after people's pets. She's been to Australia, Asia, and South America. I thought to myself, why wait until I'm in my 60s to see the world? That's when I decided to become a house- and pet-sitter. As soon as the borders opened, I left the US and have been traveling ever since. It's been the best decision in my life. The sense of freedom and discovery is immeasurable."

Harry listened attentively, absorbing the strength and resilience within Amaya's words. "That's incredible. It takes courage to follow your dreams, especially during challenging times."

A warm smile graced Amaya's face. "It's been transformative, to say the least. I've been so lucky to visit some unique places and meet wonderful people along the way. Just recently, I finished a house-sitting job in Phuket, and now I'm here on these beautiful islands, taking a breather before my next assignment in Bangkok."

"How do you support yourself, if you don't mind me asking?"

"Not at all. Before I left the country, I thought about it and took an online course in digital design. It was something that I got interested in during the lockdowns. It turned out that I have quite a talent for commercial design, but I also work on my own projects that I sell online. The other thing is that the more I travel, the more air miles I get on my credit card, so the flights get cheaper and cheaper for me."

"That's quite clever. Shall we find a place to have lunch?"

"Great idea."

They continued their journey through lush jungles and past hidden waterfalls that cascaded into emerald pools. They stopped a few times, captivated by the natural beauty surrounding them, each turn in the road revealing another marvel of the island. Back on the main road, they found a small restaurant perched on a cliff. Parking their scooters, they entered a spacious wooden terrace and settled at a table with a perfect view of the bay.

"This," Harry said, raising her glass of freshly squeezed mango juice, "is the life."

Amaya clinked her glass against Harry's. "To Koh Samui and scooter adventures," she toasted.

A few hours later, Harry and Amaya strolled along the resort's sandy paths, reminiscing about their day's adventures. Amidst the glorious bougainvillea bushes that adorned this section of the path, the two women exchanged thoughts on the remarkable meal they had shared at the beach restaurant. "The food was truly exquisite," Harry commented, a smile playing on her lips. "Thai cuisine never fails to amaze me with its freshness and powerful flavors. It's so healthy, too."

Amaya nodded, her eyes gleaming with agreement. "Absolutely! I adore Thai food. Tom yum soup and pad thai are among my favorites. And the refreshing mango sticky rice we had for dessert was to die for! It was an amazing blend of sweet and savory that really surprised me."

As their conversation dwelt on their shared experiences, Amaya suggested plans for the next day. "We should definitely go out and explore the island further," she proposed eagerly.

"Actually, tomorrow there is a boat trip to the marine reserve with lunch on the boat. It's going to be fantastic," Harry explained with excited anticipation. "Many other people are coming. You should join us."

Her curiosity piqued, Amaya asked about the other guests staying at the retreat. "I've only just met Lisa and James, and they seem nice," she said. "Who else is going?"

Harry pondered for a moment. "Well, there's Mary. She's quite friendly, although a bit ditsy at times. Apparently, she has her own yoga retreat in Spain. She's originally from Nebraska but loves to regale everyone with stories of her Eastern European heritage."

Amaya chuckled. "Sounds interesting. And what about the others?"

Harry tilted her head, thinking. "Then there's Euclid and Sarah, a couple who keep to themselves. They seem content in their own little world. We've only exchanged hellos. And then there's Anthony. He and Mary get along well, I feel, but he prefers to immerse himself in meditation. I haven't had much chance to chat with him yet."

As they reached a fork in the path, Amaya turned to bid Harry goodbye. "Well, Harry, I had a great day with you, and it's been lovely getting to know you. See you tomorrow for the boat trip," she called out, her voice carrying a warm farewell.

Harry watched as Amaya disappeared behind the hibiscus hedges. As the afternoon brought some respite from the heat, Harry decided to work outside and capture the trip and the flavors of Koh Samui for her readers. After returning to her beach hut and retrieving her laptop from inside, she sat down on the rattan armchair adorning the porch and wrote for a few hours until the automatic outdoor lights came on. It was already twilight, and with regret, Harry realized she had missed the evening yoga session. But then she looked at the screen and felt content with the work she had produced in the last few hours. Satisfied, Harry decided to close her laptop and savor the evening. She poured herself a crisp glass of Sauvignon Blanc and pulled another chair over for her to stretch her legs on while taking in her surroundings.

The Asian koel started to serenade the night, its rhythmic call luring her into a realm of cosmic tranquility. Her encounter with Amaya and the day she had spent with her exploring the island had been a welcome respite from the solitude that accompanied her frequent travels. It reminded Harry of the beauty of connecting with others.

Although she most definitely cherished the adventures and discoveries that came with her nomadic lifestyle, Harry was no stranger to the pangs of loneliness. Days would sometimes pass without her engaging in meaningful conversation, often leaving her longing for authentic human interaction. While her broad social media presence offered a semblance of connection, she found the constant craving for likes and validation from strangers to be emotionally draining. It was a relief to have temporarily severed ties to the online world during her time at the retreat.

With a contented sigh, she took another sip of her wine, immersing herself in the soothing symphony of nature. As the moon ascended even higher in the sky, illuminating the world around her, Harry reveled in the realization that her decision to leave behind the familiar confines of New York had opened doors to enchanting spectacles she might never have otherwise witnessed.

Tomorrow would bring new adventures and new faces. But for now, in the embrace of Koh Samui's serene ambiance, Harry allowed herself to be present in the now and revel in the simple joy of being alive within the empty vastness of the universe.

Harry's silent introspection was suddenly shattered by a terrible noise. Her heart raced as a piercing voice sliced through the night. Above the haunting melody of the Asian koel, a woman's screams echoed with a sense of desperation. Each cry carried the weight of anguish and confusion, leaving Harry shocked and wide-eyed.

At first she hesitated, unsure what to do, but then she put down her drink and decided to see if anyone needed help. Determined to discover the source of the fearful commotion, Harry followed the sound. She moved swiftly through the coconut trees, her steps masked by the rustling leaves overhead and the distant crash of waves against the shore. Camouflaged by the darkness, she quickly moved past Euclid and Sarah's hut. Glancing in their direction, she saw the young man comfortably spread out in the hammock on his porch, a thick, hardcover volume open somewhere in the middle resting on his chest as the young man snored gently. An empty bottle of beer was placed on the floor within arm's reach. In the opposite corner of the porch, Sarah's face was illuminated by a screen, a clear breach of the retreat's rule not to use social media. But Harry wasn't a tell-tale. With AirPods in her ears, Sarah seemed oblivious to the odd sounds outside and didn't even notice Harry as she walked past.

As Harry drew closer to where she thought the commotion was coming from, the shouts became clearer, yet their meaning remained elusive. The woman's fragmented words, like shards of a shattered puzzle, failed to form a coherent picture. "...enough..." The voice was trembling with emotion. "...always..."

As the echoes of the woman's voice faded into the night, Harry's heart felt heavy with unease. She couldn't shake off the distress she had heard in the broken and disjointed words. Her natural instinct to investigate the woman's obvious distress compelled her to take action. With the peaceful scene of Euclid and Sarah far behind her, Harry ventured deeper into the labyrinth of hibiscus hedges, guided by the moon's soft illumination. Once she emerged on the beach, she noticed a familiar figure.

Harry approached Anthony, his eyes closed in deep meditation, his face serene and peaceful amidst the chaos that had unfolded. She gently tapped his shoulder, causing him to open his eyes and break his meditative state.

"Anthony, excuse me," Harry spoke softly, her voice laced with concern. "I heard a woman's voice shouting... Is everything alright?"

Anthony sighed. "Ah, yes. It's this new couple who arrived yesterday. Lisa and... John? James? They must've had a disagreement."

Harry felt surprised. The couple didn't appear to have marital problems.

"It happens when people travel away from home and have too many drinks. The truth comes out," Anthony said stoically. "In vino veritas."

Harry's brow furrowed, a mixture of curiosity and worry knitting her features together. "It's a shame. They seem like such a happy couple."

A wistful smile played at the corners of Anthony's mouth as he leaned back, his hands resting on his knees. "Appearances can be deceiving, my dear. The masks we wear can effectively hide the battles we fight within."

Harry nodded, absorbing Anthony's seeming wisdom as her mind drifted off to ponder the oftentimes convoluted nature of human relationships.

"I see," Harry replied, her voice tinged with understanding.

Anthony placed his right hand over his heart, his eyes filled with a gentle warmth. "Indeed, my dear. It is the ebb and flow of life; the dance between harmony and discord. Now, if you'll excuse me, I prefer to meditate closer to the beach, where the whispers of the waves drown out the noise of human strife."

With a mutual nod of understanding, Harry bid Anthony goodnight. As she retreated to her hut, the weight of this newfound knowledge settled upon her shoulders like a cold shroud of apprehension. The image of a perfect family life that had captivated her just a day earlier now seemed tarnished, a mere illusion that obscured the turmoil within. The slight envy she had harbored for the couple's seemingly idyllic life was transformed into a mix of bitterness and sympathy.

Chapter 3

At Dawn

The blinding rays of the rising sun glimmer on the surface of the water. In a few hours, the shoreline will be dotted with families and couples, their laughter mingling with the whispers of the sea waves. But for now, the Koh Samui beaches are empty, the shore fringed with tall coconut palms stretching their leaves toward the sun. Paradise, at its purest. But the calm of the morning is a stark contrast to the storm swirling inside me.

I sit cross-legged, wrapped in the guise of a tourist captivated by the beauty of the moment, my gaze fixed on the horizon. Memories flood my mind, dredging up images of another time, another place.

You thought you could get away with this, didn't you?

The past—every indignity, big and small—flashes before me like a reel of old film. How many years did I endure, pretending nothing was wrong? It was time for justice. Enough was enough. The realization burns within me, each ember a memory of betrayal and hurt, wounds that have festered too long. The resentment is like poison in my veins, simmering, waiting to be released. No excuses can absolve what he did. I see his face in my mind, and it ignites a burning desire for revenge, a craving for justice that only his disappearance could satisfy.

As the sun begins to warm the wet sand, I let my mind wander through the possibilities. Koh Samui, with its natural beauty, holds so many opportunities. The sea—a perfect setting for an accident. A drowning during a snorkeling trip? But witnesses could be a problem. I weigh my options, considering the local wildlife—perhaps a venomous snake slipped into his bed. But that has too much room for error, too much chance that an innocent might get hurt.

Then, I imagine the scenic viewpoint, popular with tourists, a place where the world spreads out beneath you, deceptively close. A "tragic" fall there could pass as a simple misstep, a fatal accident while trying to snap a selfie. But no, it's too exposed. Hikers and tourists pass through, cameras ready. Someone might capture the push that sends him over the edge.

I close my eyes and take several deep breaths, letting the mantra I've come to depend on settle my mind: *Happiness is Still Possible*. After a while, I open my eyes and lie back against the sand. The sun is higher now, warming everything in sight. I glance up at the clear sky and the graceful sway of the palm fronds. And there it is—clear as day.

A perfect plan.

I don't move as the first walkers and joggers appear on the beach, resolute in my choice. The serene beauty of the sunrise and the quiet lull of the beach fill me with an odd sense of hope. *Happiness is Still Possible*. In my mind's eye, I picture the moment he realizes. The flicker of fear that will flash in his eyes. The final moment, the sweet, terrible closure to years of pain.

This plan is a masterpiece, one that can only unfold here. And as the day officially begins, I picture every move, every careful step.

"It's your last day on this planet," I whisper, barely louder than the lapping waves.

Chapter 4

The Boat Trip

The warm sea breeze caressed the guests' faces and arms as they gathered on the deck of the boat, ready for their adventure. The captain of the boat, who was also going to be their tour guide, was a cheerful local woman named Lamai.

"Good morning, everyone!" Captain Lamai's confident voice projected through the speakers. "Welcome aboard our excursion to Ang Thong National Marine Park."

The guests all nodded in eager anticipation, taking in the vivid descriptions of the attractions that awaited them with keen enthusiasm.

"We'll go to Koh Wao," Captain Lamai continued. "This is a fantastic snorkeling spot where you can marvel at the vibrant coral reefs and swim alongside a collection of colorful tropical fish."

"And, of course, we'll make a stop at Koh Mae, also known as 'Mother Island'. Here you can explore hidden caves, including the famous Tham Bua Bok or 'Lotus Cave'. Its unique stalactite formations and tranquil atmosphere make it a must-visit spot."

The guests cheered with excitement as the boat's engines roared to life, setting the stage for a day filled with exploration, relaxation, and the natural wonders of Ang Thong National Marine Park.

"Just one more thing before I forget, Yvonne asked me to remind you that when you return from your adventure, there will be a special treat awaiting you: a lovely yoga session on the beach at sunset. It'll be a perfect way to unwind after the trip."

Amaya, dressed in a bathing suit and wrapped in a black sarong, was seated beside Harry. "I love your outfit, Mary. Did you buy it on Samui?" Amaya called across the boat to Mary.

"Oh, this little thing," Mary said, pulling at her intricately embroidered Indian top with fake modesty. "I've had it for many years. I got it when I spent a year in an ashram in Rishikesh."

In her excitement, Mary started to share one of her many adventures in India. Listening with one ear, Harry looked around.

At the bow of the boat, Lisa and James reveled in the breathtaking views, capturing the moment by taking selfies and radiating joy.

"This is absolutely amazing!" James exclaimed.

Lisa, holding her cell phone up high, grinned with delight.

"You're absolutely right, James," Lisa replied, her voice full of energy.

As the boat motored further out across the azure water, conversations, laughter, and excitement continued to fill the air, creating a sense of camaraderie and anticipation among the group. Suddenly, Harry felt an unexpected wave of anxiety wash over her. Amidst the lively conversations and laughter of the guests aboard, a haunting thought infiltrated her mind: Is this how my parents spent the last day of their lives? The weight of that realization settled heavily on her chest, threatening to trigger a full-blown panic attack. She started to breathe deeply to try to control it.

Amaya, seeing Harry's distress, leaned closer.

"Harry, is everything alright? You seem troubled," she asked, her eyes reflecting genuine care.

Harry, struggling to regain control of her racing thoughts, took a few more deep breaths in an attempt to steady herself before responding to Amaya's concern.

"Yes, I'm fine now," Harry replied, her voice slightly shaky. "It's just... I suddenly thought of something very upsetting. Like a moment of déjà vu, but one that's not really mine. I'm not sure it makes sense."

Amaya reached out and clasped her hand, offering emotional support. Her touch brought a sense of grounding to Harry, and she felt a surge of gratitude for the understanding presence beside her.

"Thank you, Amaya," Harry said, her voice filled with gratitude. She wanted to explain to Amaya why she was feeling anxious, but it wasn't the right place and time. She didn't think that her fellow passengers would want to hear about boating accidents.

"You're not alone in this, Harry. I'm here to support you," Amaya whispered, sensing that there was more to Harry's sudden meltdown.

As Amaya was searching for the right words, their moment of privacy was suddenly shattered by Mary's booming voice.

"Hey, Sarah! You alright there? You're looking a bit green!"

Caught off guard by the unsolicited attention, Sarah managed a weak smile and gave a thumbs-up at Mary, signaling that she appreciated her concern.

"I'm just not a big fan of boats," Sarah admitted. "But it's important for me to face my fears. I'll be all right. As soon as we stop."

"No worries, dear; I used to be a lifeguard back in my twenties. I've got you covered!"

"Thank you, Mary. I'm just not the best when it comes to being on the water," she admitted nervously. "Euclid, on the other hand, loves everything related to the ocean. He finished his PADI course just a few days ago."

"A professional diving course! Well done! How was it?" Harry asked, curious. She had wanted to take the course but was still building up the courage.

"Fantastic! The school is not far from the retreat, so I could go there every morning. It took me five days. I'm not an expert yet, but I love being underwater in the open sea."

"I've heard that the diving courses here are very good," Harry replied, nodding. "But I can't make up my mind ... I'm afraid of sharks, you see. I'm fine snorkeling in the shallow water, but ... well... as Sarah said, we should all try to face our fears one day."

Mary seized the opportunity to ask a question that had been on her mind since she met Euclid.

"By the way, Euclid, that's quite an unusual name. Mind if I ask how you ended up with it?"

Euclid chuckled, finding amusement in recounting the story behind his name. "Well, Mary, my father happens to be a mathematics professor at Harvard," he explained. "I suppose he couldn't resist the temptation of naming his son after his favorite Greek mathematician."

Mary's eyes widened with surprise. "A mathematician's son, how interesting!" she exclaimed. "So, I take it you must be quite skilled in mathematics yourself?"

Euclid modestly nodded, acknowledging his affinity for numbers and problem-solving. "Yes. Fortunately, and staying true to my namesake, I've always had a knack for it. Currently, I teach math in Seoul, where Sarah and I live."

Lisa, holding her floppy blue hat to prevent it from flying away in the gentle breeze, decided to join the conversation.

"Is this where you met Sarah?" she inquired, her voice filled with genuine interest.

Sarah, her smile widening, responded, "Oh, no, I'm not Korean. I grew up in Chicago. I was adopted as a child."

Mary, also always eager to hear an engaging story, leaned in closer, her eyes filled with curiosity.

"Euclid and I met in Chicago on a blind date set by mutual friends."

"That's fascinating," Mary exclaimed. "So, what are you doing in Korea? It's a long way from home."

"Well, as you can imagine, I've always been obsessed with questions about my biological parents and my country of birth. My parents were very open with me about my adoption and supported my interest in Korean culture. When I was at university, I went on a study exchange to Incheon, not far from Seoul," Sarah explained, not minding Mary's nosiness. "It was a chance for me to learn more about my roots and embrace my Korean heritage. After graduating, I decided to pursue a job as an English teacher in Seoul. I've been trying to learn Korean ever since."

"That's truly amazing," Lisa chimed in. "I'm sure your Korean language skills are progressing beautifully."

"Ah, well, it's not an easy language to learn," Sarah admitted.

"You know, when I was younger, I tried to learn Polish because my grandparents were from Krakow," Mary confessed. "But, alas, I never managed to go beyond a few words and phrases."

"I can relate, Mary. I'm not exactly a linguistic genius myself," Lisa added humorously. "Though I must say, Thai sounds incredibly challenging. The Thai alphabet is simply mesmerizing to look at, but I would not want to try to learn to read it."

As the boat docked near the Emerald Lake, the guests eagerly disembarked from their boat in anticipation of the hike to the viewpoint. The dense foliage of the surrounding jungle welcomed them with cooling shade, and the sound of chirping birds filled the air. Lisa, however, hesitated at the shoreline, a pensive expression on her face.

"I think I'll stay on the beach," she announced, her voice tinged with disappointment. "My knee has been bothering me all morning. Osteoarthritis, you know."

"Are you sure you'll be alright here by yourself? I can stay with you if you'd like," James asked, concerned for his wife's well-being.

Lisa shook her head, offering a reassuring smile. "No, no, don't worry about me. I'll be fine. Besides, you shouldn't miss out on the viewpoint. It's supposed to be breathtaking. Go, enjoy it for both of us. Take some photos."

Reluctantly, James accepted Lisa's decision. With a final wave, he joined the rest of the group, making his way up the winding path to the panoramic viewpoint.

"Are you OK?" Harry asked as he caught up with the group.

"Leaving Lisa behind didn't sit well with me," James admitted, his voice tinged with concern.

Harry nodded in understanding.

"So, is it your first time in Thailand?" she asked, to take his mind off Lisa. "You both seem to enjoy it so much here."

"Oh, yes. We're having a wonderful time. This has been the best vacation we've had in over a decade."

"Oh really?" Harry imagined that James and Lisa had regularly traveled on expensive European vacations. That was the feeling she had when talking to them.

"You see since the kids were born, we've been working and saving every penny for their college. We never had the chance to venture outside the United States. But I made a good investment in the past that has recently started to pay off. And now, with the kids living on their own and us not getting any younger, we decided to see the world."

Intrigued by his words, Harry's mind began to wander, contemplating what investment had allowed James and Lisa to embark on this long-awaited adventure. She wondered if it was stock or property that gained value, but she held back from prying directly into its origin.

"Lisa insisted that we seize this opportunity before her osteoarthritis worsens," James continued, his voice filled with appreciation for his wife's determination. "We're planning to travel to Malaysia next, to a beautiful resort. From there, we'll visit various destinations in Vietnam. Perhaps you can join us if you like?"

As they strolled leisurely upwards along the verdant path, Harry's mind swirled with images of future destinations. She had been thinking of exploring these exotic countries herself.

"I wouldn't want to intrude. What are you planning to see in Malaysia?"

"Well, we're particularly excited about visiting Kuala Lumpur. It's a beautiful metropolis, from what I've seen in the photos, and Lisa loves shopping and eating out. And in Vietnam, there are so many iconic places to see! We can't wait to take the Halong Bay cruise. I booked a luxury suite on the cruise as a surprise for Lisa."

Harry thought it to be a really nice gesture from James. The image of the couple's married life was incongruous with the events of the night before. *Perhaps it wasn't Lisa and James arguing*, Harry thought to herself. As James outlined his and Lisa's plans for the rest of their vacation, she envisioned the exotic landscapes of Malaysia and Vietnam.

Soon, they reached the viewpoint. There was no mistaking the spot. Notwithstanding the other tourists busy taking photos, the view was simply breathtaking, with the shimmering waters of the lake nestled amidst the lush greenery of the surrounding hills. The group stood there, marveling at the picturesque scene.

"Harry, would you mind taking a photo of Sarah and me?" Euclid asked, extending his smartphone toward her. "I'm not a huge fan of selfies, you know. They always seem a bit pompous and smug."

Sarah playfully rolled her eyes at Euclid's comment. "Oh, come on, Euclid! Selfies can be fun. The problem is that you don't know how to take good ones."

"That's true too," Euclid conceded. "I always end up with a closeup of my forehead or nose. Trust me, no one wants to see that!"

Laughing, Harry accepted the phone and positioned herself to frame Euclid and Sarah within the stunning backdrop of the Emerald Lake. The crystal-clear water and the tropical hills formed a world-class panorama behind them.

"Alright, say *namaste*!" Harry exclaimed, capturing their beaming smiles and the majestic view in a single, well-timed snapshot.

With laughter and cheerful chatter, the rest of the group joined in by taking their own photos, each taking turns to strike humorous poses. Praise for the beauty of the surroundings filled the air.

As they descended, the excitement for the upcoming snorkeling experience was palpable. After the hike, the heat and humidity were affecting everyone, and the thought of a refreshing swim was on everyone's mind.

"I can't wait to dive into these waters!" Anthony exclaimed. "The coral reef is supposed to be second to none."

After a short boat trip filled with chatter, they anchored near Koh Wao. Again, Captain Lamai stood before them, offering important safety instructions for their snorkeling adventure.

Sarah hesitated, casting a nervous glance at the sparkling water below. Sensing her unease, Euclid offered a helping hand.

"I'll be with you every step of the way," Euclid reassured his girlfriend. "I'll teach you how to snorkel and guide you through this incredible experience. You'll see, it's going to be amazing! Do you know why you should fall backward into the water?"

"Is it so the mask stays on your face?"

"No, silly. If you fall forward from the edge of the boat, you'll end up on the floorboards in front of you."

Sarah's apprehension melted away in response to her boyfriend's corny joke.

One by one, the guests donned their snorkeling gear and entered the clear, inviting sea. Harry's heart raced with anticipation as she submerged, her eyes open to a whole new world beneath the surface.

Chapter 5

The Lotus Cave

As Harry emerged from the sea, the tantalizing aroma of grilled fish wafted through the air, mingled with the sweet scent of ripe Thai fruit and Asian spices. The boat's center table was now adorned with large plates showcasing an array of exotic tropical fruits, enticing the guests to begin a sumptuous lunch.

"You did great out there, Harry," Captain Lamai kept a light conversation with her guests.

"Thank you, and thank you for this amazing lunch! Look like heaven!"

Harry's stomach rumbled with anticipation as she imagined the taste of the perfectly grilled fish infused with aromatic Thai spices. As she quickly dried herself off with a towel, Anthony approached her discreetly, a look of unease on his face.

"Harry," Anthony whispered, his voice filled with discomfort. "Do you mind if I sit next to you during lunch? I... I just can't stand being in Lisa and James's company."

Surprised by the frank confession, Harry nodded. "Of course, Anthony."

Anthony's relief was palpable, and he gratefully took the seat next to Harry at the table, distancing himself from Lisa and James.

At that moment, Amaya, Sarah, and Mary emerged from the water, their faces glowing with a mixture of exhilaration and contentment. They quickly joined the others at the table, their towels wrapped around them for warmth.

"Oh my goodness! Look at this amazing selection of fruits!" Amaya exclaimed, her eyes sparkling with pure delight. "I can't wait to dig in. Thailand really knows how to spoil its visitors."

"I couldn't agree more," Sarah replied, her mouth watering. "These grilled fish smell divine. With all these aromatics, I'm sure they're delicious."

Mary sat next to Amaya and turned to the captain with an eager smile.

"Hey, Captain Lamai, have you ever seen a dugong in these waters?" she asked while placing some rice on her plate.

"Well, Mary, not here, but if you're lucky, there's a chance we'll spot a dugong near the shores of Koh Tan," Lamai replied. "The calm and shallow waters there provide a suitable habitat for them."

As the group savored the delicious food, the conversation naturally veered toward their recent underwater adventure.

Anthony's eyes lit up with enthusiasm.

"I love diving!" he exclaimed. "The only thing that gives me the creeps is sea snakes. The idea that they're out there makes me nervous."

Sarah's face turned pale, her eyes widening with apprehension.

"Sea snakes?" she stammered. "I had no idea! I wouldn't have jumped into the water if I knew they were around."

"Don't worry," the captain reassured everyone. "Sea snakes are not common where we are now. You're perfectly safe here. They are typically found in rocky areas and steep cliffs. We're far away from their usual habitat."

The conversation then shifted to the spiciness of the food, with Lisa expressing her concern.

"Sarah, can you tell me whether that sauce is really spicy?" she asked. "I've had some extremely hot food since I arrived in Thailand, something that has taken me by surprise."

Sarah chuckled, recalling her own experiences with Thai spice.

"It depends on your tolerance, Lisa," Sarah replied with a smile. "Just be cautious if you're not used to it. And hey, don't worry, your head won't explode like Mary's did with that chili!"

Mary joined in the laughter, amused at her misadventures with spicy food.

"Oh, yes!" she recalled, laughing. "That grilled chili incident at dinner two nights ago was one I will never forget. I nearly turned into a fire-breathing dragon, and I couldn't catch my breath! My whole face turned red, even my ears! Lesson learned: Always double-check your food before taking a bite."

The group erupted in laughter, their bond growing stronger as they shared amusing anecdotes and relished the joys of their Thai adventure.

As they reached the next destination, Tham Bua Bok, or 'Lotus Cave', everyone stirred from their peaceful reverie. Lisa, once again plagued by her osteoarthritis, decided to remain on the boat. James opted to keep her company, content to sit there together and soak up the beauty of the surroundings. The rest of the group, eager for exploration, ventured inside the mysterious cave.

Slender stalactites hung gracefully from the ceiling while somewhat fatter stalagmites rose from the cave floor, forming otherworldly shapes that seemed to stand guard over ancient secrets.

"Oh gosh! These really look like blossoming lotus flowers! Now I realize why it's called the Lotus Cave!" Mary kept on pointing at the various features of the rock formations, not allowing anyone time to reflect or admire them in peace.

As other guests drifted away from Mary, Harry, curious about the subtle tension between Anthony and James, seized the opportunity to ask her about it.

"I couldn't help but notice that Anthony seems distant around James. Is there a reason for that?"

Mary paused, her gaze drifting momentarily to Anthony, who was contemplating the cave entrance from afar.

"Well, it's a complicated matter, really." Mary looked around to make sure that James couldn't overhear her. "You see, Anthony lost his life savings in a pyramid scheme. He trusted his high school best friend with his money, and the friend invested heavily in the scheme, only to find out later that it was a scam. It's been an incredibly difficult time for him. That's why he despises financial advisors of any kind, especially when they are flaunting their good fortune and money as much as James does."

Harry's eyes widened, understanding the weight of Anthony's loss.

"That's terrible. How old is Anthony?"

Mary pondered for a moment, estimating his age.

"I believe he's around sixty. It's devastating to have to start from scratch at that age. Anthony's resilience is commendable. I can't imagine having to face such adversity."

"It must take incredible strength to bounce back from such a setback. Is that why he's here in Thailand?"

"Indeed; he's borrowed some money to come here and explore some new business ideas," Mary replied, her voice filled with admiration for Anthony's determination. "He's considering opening a small hotel and retiring in this paradise. I think he sees it as a chance for a fresh start; a way to rebuild his life."

The atmosphere abruptly shifted as Anthony playfully sneaked up on the two women, his voice filled with joviality.

"Ah, caught you two red-handed! Have you been gossiping about me?"

Harry and Mary's faces flushed with embarrassment, fearing they had been overheard. Mary, adopting a conspiratorial tone, decided to come clean.

"Well, Anthony, we were just discussing why you don't particularly care for James. I didn't mean to be a gossip; I was just explaining things for Harry," Mary whispered.

Anthony, his playful demeanor fading for a moment, looked at Harry with a mixture of seriousness and understanding.

"I apologize if I came across as judgmental. But it's true; I have a deep aversion to anyone who profits from investing other people's hard-earned savings into unsound schemes. It's a matter of principle for me."

Before the conversation could continue, they were interrupted by the arrival of the others, their voices echoing through the cavern.

"Wow, look at these stunning stalactites! It's like nature's own chandelier," Sarah announced.

Euclid, always eager to share his knowledge, chimed in.

"Did you know that Tham Bua Bok cave is said to be home to a unique species of blind cavefish? They've adapted perfectly to the darkness and lack of natural light."

As the group absorbed this newfound information, a sudden, deafening bang echoed throughout the cave, reverberating against the walls.

The guests froze. As their initial shock subsided, Harry's eyes darted to Anthony, who remained frozen, his complexion drained of color. At his feet lay the broken remains of a massive stalactite, the cause of the thunderous sound when it crashed on the ground.

The group's attention shifted to Anthony. With no time to waste, Mary was by his side, bombarding him with a flurry of questions.

"Anthony, are you okay? Did any rock fragments hit you? Are you feeling dizzy or in pain?" she inquired.

"You know, even a small object falling from a great height can be lethal. Anthony could have been killed," Euclid was quick to analyze the situation.

As they made their somber way back to the boat, Harry couldn't help but ponder the unfortunate circumstances surrounding Anthony. She turned to Amaya, who was walking beside her.

"Anthony must have really bad luck. What are the chances?"

"Perhaps it's karma. Sometimes, life has a way of balancing things out. Let's hope his luck takes a turn for the better."

On the way back, Harry found herself sitting with Lisa, James, and Amaya, marveling at the picturesque view of the passing islands.

"Look at the islands passing by," Harry said, her tone filled with admiration. "They seem like nature's masterpieces, each with their own unique charm. Do you know the names of any of them?"

They spent a few minutes chatting with the captain about the various islands.

"The boat trip reminds me of the time I used to accompany Clara on sailing competitions," Lisa said, a nostalgic tone coloring her words. "She was quite the sailor, you know. She even won several important competitions."

"That's very impressive," Amaya remarked. "Is Clara your only child?"

"No, we also have a son, Chris, but he's not a great sailor. He's into science."

Lisa beamed with pride as she shared her children's accomplishments.

"Chris is studying medicine at Harvard Medical School. It's one of the most prestigious medical institutions in the US. He wants to become a renowned brain surgeon."

"A brain surgeon! That's a tremendous goal."

Lisa smiled and replied, "Yes, that's true. It's not uncommon for brain surgeons to earn a good six-figure salary, or even more."

Harry, although she had tried her best to maintain polite interest in the conversation, couldn't help but feel detached as Lisa recounted her children's achievements once again. She admired Lisa's pride in their success but couldn't shake the feeling that Lisa was living life vicariously through them.

"Your children have certainly set a high bar for themselves," Harry complimented. "But what about you? What makes you tick?"

Lisa's gaze drifted away, seemingly caught off guard by Harry's direct question. After a moment of hesitation, she reached for the champagne bottle, pouring the last round of bubbly into their glasses.

"You know, I haven't really shared this with many people," she said, beginning to open up. "But I've been secretly taking art lessons. It's something I've always wanted to do. Ever since elementary school I have had a knack for painting, and a deep love for art in general. But life took me along a different pathway, and I had to put my artistic dreams on hold."

"That's wonderful, Lisa!" Harry's exclaimed sincerely. "What kind of art do you enjoy creating?"

Lisa's face brightened with a newfound sense of enthusiasm as she shared her artistic journey.

"I've been exploring different mediums and techniques," she explained, her voice brimming with passion. "Experimenting with acrylics and mixed media has been fascinating. I hope to convert one of the children's old bedrooms into a studio. My dream is to create beautiful pieces and maybe even start selling my artwork in the future."

"That sounds incredible, Lisa," Harry said.

Amaya agreed. "It takes courage to pursue your passions. I have no doubt you'll be a great success. If you ever need a sounding board or advice on how to promote it, count me in. I've been selling my art online and have suffered a few mishaps I could help you avoid."

As the conversation about Lisa's artistic aspirations unfolded, James couldn't resist interjecting.

"Oh, Amaya, that's very kind of you, but we're unlikely to see any money from Lisa's art," he remarked, his voice dripping with condescension.

Lisa, feeling indignant at James's hurtful comment, couldn't let it slide without a response. "Well, James, let me remind you that Van Gogh himself died in poverty, and yet his paintings are now worth millions."

"Honey, I love you, but you're no Van Gogh."

Everyone fell silent, astounded at James's rude remarks about his wife's artistic endeavors. Lisa strode away toward the back of the boat. The uncomfortable silence that followed lingered for a moment as Harry and Amaya exchanged uneasy glances.

"You know, when it comes to amateur art, sometimes your family and friends are the only ones who will tell you the truth," James said to Harry and Amaya, in an effort to break the tension. "I'm just trying to spare my wife disappointment and humiliation."

Amaya and Harry nodded politely while lost in their own thoughts. Returning to the enchanting island of Koh Samui, Harry stood at the bow of the boat, taking in the breathtaking view. The island's lush greenery formed the backdrop to several pristine beaches. Coconut palm trees swayed gently in the warm breeze, casting their elongated shadows over the powdery sand. Koh Samui appeared as a haven of tranquility, a place where one could escape the bustle of everyday life.

"Welcome back!" they were greeted by Yvonne, who was standing at the entrance to the jetty with a tray of glasses. "Our chef has prepared special detox mocktails for you to get you ready for the session. They contain ginger, turmeric and honey—antioxidant and anti-inflammatory," she explained as she handed each guest a small glass filled with an orange liquid.

"This is wonderful!" Mary exclaimed as she lifted her glass. "Cheers, everyone."

"I'm glad you like it," Yvonne smiled. "I'll see you all soon on the beach. Bring your mats."

Chapter 6

A Suspicious Incident

The guests set their mats in a line, facing the horizon. Harry settled into a comfortable position on her yoga mat, her eyes closed. The sunset mindfulness session was her favorite part of the day at the retreat. Yvonne was right behind them, guiding them in their meditation. The rhythmic sound of waves crashing against the shore filled the air, harmonizing with the rustling leaves overhead and the chirping of the small birds living in the coconut palms behind her.

"Take a deep breath in, feeling the coolness of the air entering your lungs," Yvonne said, her soft voice resonating. "As you exhale, release any tension or worries, allowing your body to sink deeper into relaxation."

As the session progressed, Yvonne's voice became even more soothing. "With every breath, you find yourself more open, more receptive. Your thoughts, like leaves floating on the surface of a river, drift away, leaving a calm, clear space within. This space is open, ready to embrace new ideas and new directions. Imagine this openness as a door, allowing entry to only what benefits you, guiding you to make choices that align with your deepest desires and well-being."

Yvonne continued, her words remaining soft but deliberate, "As you breathe in, think of peace; breathe out any hesitation. You are in control, yet open to exploring new paths and new ways of seeing the world around you. Trust in this journey, knowing you are guided by a deep inner wisdom."

Harry followed Yvonne's prompts, as the instructor's words floated on the gentle breeze, blending seamlessly with the sounds of nature, and she felt the ebb and flow of her breath syncing with the rise and fall of the waves. The air carried a hint of salt mingled with the subtle scents of coconut and frangipani. She was grounded in the present moment.

"Now, shift your attention to the sensations in your body," Yvonne said. "Notice any areas of tightness or discomfort. Send your breath to those places, releasing tension and inviting a sense of ease to replace any pain you might feel."

Harry let her awareness explore the intricate landscape of the myriad sensations residing within her body. With each breath, she felt a subtle release; a gentle unfurling and loosening of her muscles as if nature itself was guiding her toward a state of equilibrium.

"Listen to the sounds around you. Hear the waves crashing, the rustling leaves, and the birdsong. Allow these sounds to anchor you and your breathing in the present, connecting you to the essence of this very moment."

Harry concentrated on Yvonne's words, letting each wave of sound gently carry away her lingering thoughts. Immersed in the symphony of nature, she found solace and serenity in its harmonious melody.

"Now, as the sun descends below the horizon, imagine its warm afterglow bathing you in a peaceful farewell. Feel its fading golden light infuse every cell of your being, nurturing and revitalizing your spirit."

Harry visualized the sun's slow, inexorable descent, its final rays enveloping her like a soft, cozy blanket. She fed from its nourishing energy, allowing it to fill her with a renewed sense of vitality and inner peace, ready to face the darkness. As the sun set, the air fell still, and the guests found themselves enveloped in silence.

At that instant, Harry felt well and truly grounded and centered. It was a moment of quiet reflection; a moment in time when she could connect with herself and the world around her. As the sun abandoned the sky and left the group in twilight, she felt a sense of determination regarding the journey that lay ahead.

"I'm going to find out what really happened," she said, making a quiet promise to the ghosts from her past before taking a deep breath.

Just as Harry was about to exhale, a panicked voice pierced the air, jolting her back to reality.

"Help! Help! Anyone!"

Harry's eyes flew open, and she immediately noticed that Yvonne was already on the move in the direction that Marieke was calling from. Running surprisingly swiftly, Yvonne dashed along the sandy path that led toward the coconut plantation.

Turning her gaze toward her companions, Harry saw that they had all remained in mindfulness postures, shocked by the sudden cries for help and unable to act. As the urgency of the situation began to unfold, Harry felt a surge of adrenaline course through her veins. She stood up, understanding that something terrible must have happened.

Lisa, bewildered, directed her questioning gaze at the others.

"We should go and see if we can help," Anthony suggested, his voice steady and determined.

Nodding in agreement, Harry and the rest of the group quickly followed Anthony's lead, their footsteps rapid as they made their way toward the place where Marieke's distressed cries had originated. Harry's heart pounded in anticipation of what they might find.

As the group reached the coconut plantation, they saw Marieke and Yvonne kneeling on the ground, their eyes filled with despair. James lay lifeless on the ground, motionless against the backdrop of the palm trees. Lisa's piercing shriek of anguish shattered the air as she rushed toward them, her voice trembling with fear and disbelief.

"What happened? James!" Lisa cried out, her voice cracking with despair.

Marieke, her voice choked with tears, pointed to the gash on the back of James's head. She could only speculate that a random falling coconut had struck him, causing a fatal injury.

Lisa whimpered softly, repeating the words, "I'm so sorry," in a broken tone. The weight of the tragedy hung heavily in the air, suffocating the once-peaceful atmosphere.

Amidst the chaos and grief, Mary pushed past the crowd, taking charge of the situation. With a commanding voice, she instructed Marieke to call an ambulance, urgency punctuating her words. Marieke, trembling, nodded and quickly retrieved her cell phone.

Mary kneeled down beside James, her experienced eyes scanning his still form. With methodical precision, she began checking for signs of life.

First, she gently placed her fingertips on James's carotid artery on the side of his neck, just below his jawline. She pressed lightly, her touch sensitive and calibrated, but James's skin remained motionless, and she felt no reassuring throb beneath her fingertips that would indicate a beating heart.

Undeterred, Mary shifted her attention to James's wrist, feeling for his radial artery. Her fingers pressed lightly against the skin, feeling for any sign of life coursing through his veins. The seconds stretched out, elongated by the uncertainty that hung in the air. With gentle pressure, she located the spot just below the base of his thumb. She pressed her fingers against the skin, but again found no trace of life.

Marieke, her voice quivering, relayed the distressing news to the emergency services on the other end of the line. It felt like an eternity as the group stood in stunned silence, their hearts heavy with the weight of the unfolding tragedy.

Mary knew there was no time to waste. Her trained instincts kicked into high gear.

"We need to act quickly!" Mary's voice carried a mix of urgency and determination as she shouted to everyone.

Without hesitation, and with focus and skill, she placed the heel of her palm on the center of James's chest and overlaid her other hand on top. Interlocking her fingers, she positioned herself directly over James.

Harnessing her upper body strength, Mary began to deliver firm and consistent compressions, pushing down with enough force to depress the chest.

"I think someone will have to take over soon," she spoke as she maintained a steady rhythm that mirrored the beat of a healthy heart. "I'm too old for this, I fear."

Euclid, who had just arrived at the scene, volunteered and, following Mary's instructions to the letter, took over the CPR.

As Euclid diligently performed the chest compressions, Mary started artificial ventilation. After each set of 30 compressions, she leaned forward, carefully pinched James's nose shut and created an airtight seal over his mouth with her own. With a firm exhale, she delivered two rescue breaths, observing the rise and fall of his chest.

Mary then instructed Sarah how to stop the bleeding. Sarah removed her sarong and applied it firmly to the wound on the back of James's head. Mary checked it to make sure she exerted gentle pressure, ensuring that James would not lose any more precious blood.

The scene unfolded in a blur of urgency and teamwork. Euclid and Mary continued the rhythmic cycles of chest compressions and rescue breaths, maintaining a steady tempo as Mary poured her skill and determination into reviving James. The group watched with bated breath, their collective hopes pinned on Mary's efforts, as they prayed for a positive outcome in this race against time.

The wailing sirens grew louder, signaling the imminent arrival of the ambulance. Moments later, a team of Thai paramedics appeared by James's body. Euclid, his hands trembling slightly from the exertion of providing CPR, stepped back to allow the paramedics to take over. They had done everything they could to stabilize James, and now it was time for the experts to continue giving him medical care.

With swift efficiency, the paramedics assessed James's condition, assessing vital signs and exchanging brief but crucial information with one another. Their calm demeanor and clear communication revealed their experience in handling critical situations.

One paramedic positioned himself at James's head, carefully stabilizing his neck and spine, while the others prepared the stretcher and other equipment necessary for his transport. Their synchronized movements and coordinated efforts showcased their expertise and dedication to saving lives.

Mary, her face etched with a mix of exhaustion and concern, approached Lisa, who stood at the edge of the unfolding scene, her eyes filled with fear and desperation. Mary placed a reassuring hand on Lisa's shoulder, offering comfort and support.

"I'm so sorry." Lisa kept on repeating the apology. "When we were getting ready for the session, I was still angry at him for his comments on the boat. I told him to go to hell... These were my last words to him." Tears were streaming down her face

"Lisa, it's not your fault. Stop thinking about it. James will be fine," Mary said decisively, her voice filled with empathy. "The paramedics will take over and do everything they can for James. You should go to the hospital with them. Marieke said she'll meet you there to help translate."

Lisa nodded, her voice choked with emotion. She clung to Mary, seeking support before turning her attention to the paramedics who were carefully maneuvering the stretchers toward James. With tear-filled eyes, Lisa followed them.

As the paramedics expertly loaded James onto the stretcher and prepared to transport him to the nearest trauma ward, a cacophony of sirens pierced the air once more. The urgency of the situation hung heavy, casting a somber atmosphere over the retreat. With a shared resolve and silent prayers, the group watched as the ambulance sped away.

Darkness fell as scudding rain clouds blanked out the feeble stars above. Time seemed to stand still, suspended in the wake of the tragic event that had unfolded before them.

Chapter 7

SHADOWS OF SERENITY

Seated in the dimly lit restaurant, and with a storm raging outside, the group found comfort in each other's company. The sound of heavy rain drumming against the windows mingled with the distant rumble of thunder was a reminder of the tempestuous night that had befallen Koh Samui.

The retreat's restaurant, nestled on the beachfront, boasted panoramic views of the sea. Through the rain-streaked windows, Harry saw the waves crashing against the shore, their wild dance illuminated by occasional flashes of lightning. Orchid flowers adorned the tables, their bright colors adding an incongruent touch of tropical elegance to the tense atmosphere.

A waitress approached the group with a warm smile. She skillfully balanced a tray of cocktails on one hand. The tantalizing aromas of Thai spices and fruits wafted through the air, a testament to the culinary delights that awaited within the restaurant's kitchen.

"Here are your drinks," the waitress said, her voice barely audible above the wind howling outside. "Who ordered Mai Tai?"

Sarah and Mary waved their hands to indicate that the cocktails were theirs.

"That looks amazing!" Sarah picked up her drink and admired the elaborate presentation. "It's the first time I'm having it. What's in it?"

"Our Mai Tais are made with rum, orange liqueur, and tropical fruit juice. I hope you enjoy it! The Basil Mojitos are for you?" The waitress placed the drink in front of Harry and Anthony.

Harry nodded and admired the zesty color of her drink.

"Then the strawberry daiquiri is for you," she added, presenting Amaya's drink. "And one Chang beer for you."

"Thank you." Euclid grabbed the small beer can and poured its contents into an ice-frosted glass.

The waitress paused for a moment, surveying the weary faces of the group before continuing, "Is there anything else I can assist you with? Our kitchen is still open, and we have a variety of dishes available if you are hungry."

Everyone in the group politely declined, their minds preoccupied with thoughts of James. The weight of the situation had stolen their appetites, leaving them with only a sense of unease.

"That's very kind of you to offer," Harry replied. "But for now, we'll just wait for any news from the hospital. Thank you."

The waitress nodded. "Of course. I'll be here if you need anything. Take your time, and I hope everything turns out well."

With a final smile, she retreated to the restaurant's kitchen area, leaving the group to their thoughts. The soft glow of candlelight danced upon their faces, casting flickering shadows of uncertainty around the table. Everyone was trying to process the events of the day in their own way, from the idyllic boat trip to the unfortunate accident.

As Harry sipped her drink, her thoughts turned to the incident and how strange it was, but it was Euclid who, ever the skeptic, raised the topic for discussion.

"You know, I've been thinking of James's accident and how unusual it was. But it turns out such things not as uncommon as I thought. It was bothering me, so I looked it up online before I came here. The article I read says that more people die from falling coconuts than from shark attacks. It might be an urban legend, but I wonder if there's any truth to it."

"Really?" Sarah was intrigued by the notion. "That's quite a claim. But if it's an urban legend, there must be some basis for it, right? I mean, coconuts are pretty heavy, and if they happen to fall from a significant height..."

Euclid nodded, his mind engaged in this peculiar debate. "Exactly! Coconuts can weigh up to four pounds, and if they were to plummet from a tall tree, they could certainly cause some damage. But I couldn't find any statistics on this. I may look again later."

"I think it was a case of being in the wrong place at the wrong time," Amaya interjected. "By the way, what was James doing walking across the plantation during the mindfulness session?"

"Oh, I don't think he was feeling well," Harry commented. "He told me before the session that he had an upset stomach. I thought he might have had heat exhaustion but he insisted on taking part in the session."

"That's true. I heard him complain about his stomach," Sarah said. "He must have felt worse and decided to head back to his hut."

"I think there should be a sign warning people not to walk under the coconuts," Mary reflected. "It's so dangerous."

"But you know... whether it's statistically likely or not that James was hit by a coconut, if you weren't there, I don't think I could have revived him. Let's drink to Mary," Anthony remarked, sipping his mojito.

Everyone raised their glasses. "To Mary!"

Mary blushed at the unexpected praise. "Oh, it was just instinct. I'm surprised I remembered my first aid training from my lifeguard years. But they say it's like riding a bike, right? Once you learn it, it sticks with you."

Sarah smiled warmly at Mary. "Well, thank goodness you did remember. Your quick actions were incredible. You saved his life."

As the time passed, the conversation became stilted. There was still no news from the hospital, but as it was getting late and the staff wanted to close the restaurant for the night, the group decided to call it a day and head back to their respective huts.

They made their way through the darkened coconut plantation, guided by the soft glow of solar spotlights and lanterns hanging from the trees. A break in the storm had granted them temporary respite from the heavy rain. The damp earth beneath their feet clung to their flip-flops, and everyone's heart was heavy with worry and anxiety.

In the distance, beyond the resort's boundary line, the chorus of the jungle came alive. The haunting call of coucals resonated through the night air, casting a somber note over their short journey.

Harry walked beside Amaya. The darkness enveloped them, punctuated only by intermittent glimmers of the lights and the distant sounds of the jungle. She couldn't help but feel a shiver of unease crawl up her spine as they walked past the site where the accident had happened.

"I don't want to look at the spot where we found James," Harry confessed. "It's too unsettling."

Amaya nodded in agreement. "I don't blame you. But look," she said, pointing to the ground. "The rain has washed away the blood. It's as if nothing ever happened."

Relieved by Amaya's observation, Harry mustered a faint smile. "You're right. It's a small comfort amidst all of this uncertainty. It seems that the Earth keeps on spinning no matter what happens—hopefully tomorrow, things will look brighter."

As they approached the crossroads leading to the various huts, it was time to say goodbye. The soothing sound of crashing waves on the beach nearby reached their ears, blending with the whispers of the coconut palm leaves.

"I'm sure we'll find out about James in the morning," Mary said, her voice carrying a note of reassurance. "Let's get some rest and hope for the best."

They bade each other goodnight. The weight of the day's events lingered in the air, casting a passing shadow over their kind farewells. Harry entered her hut, closed the door behind her, and took a moment to breathe. The room felt like a cocoon; a shelter from the uncertainties of life that swirled around chaotically outside.

As she settled into her bed, she listened to the sound of the rain returning, pattering against the wooden veranda and the windows with renewed vigor. The thatched roof dampened its fury. As Harry sought comfort within the warm ambiance of her hut, she tried to silence the wave of anxiety that was building inside her. James's accident had triggered many emotions that Harry was struggling to deal with, including the realization of how fleeting life is. Tomorrow would bring answers, she hoped, and a glimmer of optimism clung to her weary heart. As she was about to drift into sleep, she heard a knock on the door. On the porch was Marieke, soaking wet from the storm raging behind her.

"Marieke! Come in," Harry said, rushing her inside. "What are you doing here? Have you got any news about James?" She handed Marieke a clean towel to dry her face and hair.

"He's in a coma." Marieke's voice trembled as she spoke, her tone heavy with anguish. She slumped into a seat.

"Oh no!" Harry sat down on an armchair opposite Marieke. "What did the doctors say?"

"They don't know when or if he'll ever wake up." Marieke took a deep breath, trying to steady herself, then she remembered something. "Do you have a glass?" She pulled a bottle of whiskey from her handbag.

"Yes, of course," Harry said, fetching some. Marieke poured them both generous measures.

While Harry sipped her drink, Marieke finished hers in one go and topped it up again.

"Sorry to bother you so late at night, Harry, but I had to speak to someone. It's like a nightmare. The worst thing that could have happened to this business. If James does not recover, we'll be ruined. 'Death at a Yoga Retreat'..." Marieke said, pretending to read an imaginary newspaper headline.

"And how is Lisa? How did she take the news?" Harry inquired.

Marieke recounted the heartbreaking scene at the hospital. "It was unbearable, Harry. When the doctors broke the news to Lisa, she couldn't contain her grief. She was wailing, crying uncontrollably. It was as if her world had shattered into a million pieces."

Harry's heart ached at the thought of Lisa's anguish, imagining the pain she must be going through. "I can't even begin to fathom what she's experiencing," Harry whispered, her voice filled with empathy.

Marieke nodded. "She was so overwhelmed that they had to give her something to calm her down, just to help her cope with the news. I wanted her to come back to the retreat, but she insisted on staying at the hospital in case James woke up. I organized a guest bed for her and then called her daughter to break the news. Lisa herself was not able to speak. She just sat there staring blankly into the distance. I think it was the drugs they gave her. She was quite peaceful when I left her, but lost in her own world."

"Her children must be devastated," Harry said softly, her voice filled with compassion.

Marieke's eyes glistened. "I spoke to Clara, the daughter, and she's going to inform her brother. She was quite devastated and said she was going to make arrangements to come here as soon as possible. Lisa will need her family by her side during this difficult time."

At that moment, Harry realized the magnitude of the support Lisa would require in the coming days. "We have to be there for her, Marieke," Harry said firmly, her voice filled with determination. "Not just for Lisa, but for James and their children, too. They need us."

"Thank you, Harry. It's really helped to talk to someone and to share this burden."

Leaning back in her armchair, Harry's mind again swirled with thoughts and emotions. She wondered why Marieke came to her first. Why wasn't she recounting the events at the hospital to her wife? There was something more to Marieke's surprise night visit. Harry decided to probe gently.

"Is there anything else that's bothering you?"

Marieke took a deep breath, steadying herself before speaking. "It's about the incident: the coconut. I don't think it was an accident."

Harry's brows furrowed, her mind trying to process Marieke's words. "What do you mean? Are you suggesting someone staged it?"

Marieke's gaze grew intense, her voice filled with a mixture of fear and determination. "I don't know, Harry. I've been thinking, going over everything in my mind. It's just... it all seems too strange. The approaching storm, the coconut, the timing. It's like someone wanted to harm James and knew that the storm would destroy any evidence."

Harry's eyes widened, a chill coursing through her veins. "Are you saying someone intentionally caused the coconut to fall?"

Marieke shook her head, her voice barely above a whisper. "Of course, you can't just make coconuts fall off a tree, but something is off."

Marieke's hands trembled slightly as she poured herself another shot of whiskey. The weight of the information she held was evident in her eyes as she looked at Harry, her voice filled with a mixture of anxiety and determination.

"Harry, I need to tell you something, but you mustn't tell anyone else," she began, her words punctuated by a deep sigh. "After I came back from the hospital, I went back to the place where James was struck. I wanted to understand what had happened and to find the coconut that hit him. It was dark so I used a torch to look for it. That's when I saw a metal object in the hibiscus bush, not far from where we discovered James's body. It was a big hammer. There were specks of blood on it." Marieke paused to let Harry digest this information.

"What? Are you saying that someone tried to kill James by hitting him on the head with a hammer?" Harry couldn't believe what she was hearing.

"Yes, I know it sounds surreal, and I do not want to believe the insinuation. But the evidence is the evidence." Marieke's voice shuddered as the implications of what had just been disclosed began to settle in.

Harry's eyes widened in disbelief, her mind racing. "A bloodied hammer?" she repeated, her voice filled with a mix of astonishment and concern. "Marieke, are you saying someone deliberately staged the attack on James to make it appear like an accident?"

Marieke nodded, tears streaming down her face. "Yes, that's what I believe," she replied, her voice quivering with unease. "It seems that someone wanted it to look like James was hit by a falling coconut, but they miscalculated. They didn't anticipate that there would be someone nearby able to revive him, and that I would find the murder weapon."

Harry felt both bewilderment and apprehension. The talk of evidence and attempted murder took her back to her first reporting job for a small newspaper in her hometown, Ithaca. She hadn't been a crime reporter per se because Ithaca, being a small town, did not have a need for a dedicated investigative reporter, but on the few occasions when something terrible happened in the town, she had been tasked with reporting on it for the newspaper's readers.

The few murders that she had written about were driven by greed and envy; there was nothing out of the ordinary about them. But here, on this peaceful island, she found it hard to imagine the motive. Yes, James was not a perfect human being; he didn't always seem supportive of his wife, and he might have upset people in his job as a financial advisor, but nobody was perfect. Would any of these be enough motive to kill? She couldn't fathom why anyone would want to harm James or why they would go to such lengths to plan the attempted murder. The idyllic retreat she had come to enjoy had become a place of danger and mystery.

"I can't believe someone would do this," Harry said, her voice filled with a mix of unease and determination. "We need to find out who would want to harm James and why. We can't let them get away with this."

"I hoped you'd say that. That's why I came to you first," Marieke said, wiping her tears, her resolve strengthening. "We need to find out the truth, not only for James and his family, but to save this place from ruin."

Harry nodded. She wasn't sure how she and Marieke were to go about investigating the attack, but she was willing to help.

Inside the warm confines of Harry's hut, the sound of the howling wind and rain lashing against the windows filled the air. The dim glow of tealights illuminated their faces as they set on a journey to find a murderer.

"We need to be cautious, though," Marieke continued. "Whoever did this may still be among us, watching and waiting."

"I agree. Whoever did it knew James well and harbored a grudge against him. They could be one of the guests at the retreat. Have you called the police?" Harry asked, her voice laced with concern. "We need to tell them about the bloodied hammer. It could be a vital piece of evidence."

Marieke's gaze dropped, her fingers tracing circles on the rim of her glass. With a heavy sigh, she confessed, "I didn't call the police, Harry. In fact, I wanted to throw the hammer into the sea the moment I found it, but then I had doubts. What if it really is a murder weapon? What if there is a police investigation? I'd go to prison for destroying evidence."

Harry couldn't believe what she was hearing. "It was good you didn't throw it away. It could be crucial to finding out what happened to James. There might be fingerprints or the attacker's DNA on the handle. You should take it to the police."

Marieke's voice wavered as she struggled to explain. "It's... it's complicated, Harry. I've hidden it away. We can't have Thai police involved in this."

"I don't understand."

"It has something to do with Yvonne. I have to protect her."

"Yvonne? What does she have to do with all of this?"

Marieke shifted her body forward, her voice barely above a whisper. "Yvonne... she has a dark past; one I'll share with you, but only in confidence."

Harry's eyes widened. "What is it?"

Marieke took a deep breath. "When Yvonne was in her early twenties, she was caught trying to smuggle cocaine from Bangkok to Amsterdam. It was a terrible mistake, Harry. She was manipulated by her boyfriend at the time and tricked into being a drug mule. Yvonne paid a heavy price for that mistake. She spent several years in a Thai prison, her innocent youth stripped away."

Harry's mind whirled with shock and compassion. The revelation offered a glimpse into the depths of Yvonne's past, explaining her guarded nature and fear of law enforcement. "I had no idea, Marieke. That must have been an incredibly difficult time for Yvonne."

Marieke concurred. "It was a nightmare, Harry. Yvonne finally gained her freedom in her thirties through a prison amnesty program. It was a miracle that she was able to leave. She's worked so hard since then to rebuild her life and find happiness and peace. I can't allow the Thai police to become involved in James's accident. If they start searching the retreat, they might uncover some marijuana or other drugs that some of the guests or staff have. I can't control what people do here in the privacy of their accommodations—but even a small joint would send her back to that hellish place."

A heavy silence settled between them; the consequences of what Yvonne might face if an official police investigation went awry justified Marieke's actions to a degree. Harry understood the difficult position Marieke found herself in, torn between seeking justice for James and protecting the woman she loved.

The rain pelting against the windows and the howling wind outside began to subside. Harry had a lot of questions about Yvonne's past, questions that she felt she needed answered before she ventured on the journey to find James's killer.

"Why didn't Yvonne go back home to the Netherlands after she was released from prison?" Harry asked softly. "If it were me, I would not want anything to do with this country. I've read of people being sent to jail for decades for what would be a small infringement in the US."

Marieke sighed, her gaze wandering into the past. "It's hard to explain, Harry. Yvonne's time in prison was a truly terrible experience. She hardly ever speaks of it, but I know it scarred her deeply."

Harry nodded, her expression empathetic and understanding. "I can only imagine."

"For almost a decade, she was confined to a cramped cell with little to no privacy. The overcrowding was unbearable, and basic necessities were scarce. The heat and humidity were oppressive, and the lack of proper ventilation made it suffocating for her and her fellow inmates. The daily routine was grueling, filled with physical labor and monotony. It was a place that broke spirits."

Harry's heart ached for Yvonne as she tried to grasp the horrors she must have seen during her time behind bars. "She must have felt hopeless, thinking she would be in her forties by the time she was released."

Marieke nodded, her eyes brimming with sadness. "Exactly, Harry. Yvonne lost hope during those long years. Within weeks of being locked up, her best friend in Amsterdam stopped writing to her. Her other so-called friends were tied to the boyfriend who got her involved in smuggling in the first place. He disappeared from the face of the earth—must have changed his name, I suppose, fearing that Yvonne would rat on him and his gang. The Thai police checked the address that Yvonne gave them, but they found nothing at the rented villa. It was abandoned, and the name on the lease turned out to be a woman whose identity had been stolen."

"What about her family? Didn't they miss her?"

"She never had a good relationship with her father; they hadn't talked in years when she got locked up, and he never even wrote to her. Not once! And her poor mother died of breast cancer while Yvonne was in jail."

A brief silence settled between them as Harry thought of Yvonne's tragic life story. So much sadness and misery before she was 30 years old. "When Yvonne finally left prison after serving ten years, she had no one to turn to. She had literally nothing but the clothes on her back. She had no work experience and no contacts in the job market. She was completely lost. But you know... my wife is a very strong woman. She reinvented herself and started from nothing. Thailand had become her home, even though it was the place that had held her captive. She could speak Thai fluently, and it was all she knew. There was nothing for her in Amsterdam."

"It's remarkable. What did she do?"

"When she was in jail, she used to spend hours meditating. It was her way of coping with the nightmare; a mental escape. She also practiced yoga and mindfulness to help her body get through the stress. So, when she was out of jail, she would go from resort to resort, working part-time with holidaymakers. When you work casually, employers are not too interested in your past. It also helped that she was from Europe and spoke perfect English. Guests loved her, and so she focused on alternative treatments. She took courses in hypnotherapy and reiki. She also studied herbal medicine and massage therapy."

"It's true, Yvonne does have a gift for alternative healing," Harry said. Yvonne's meditation and mindfulness sessions were the best she had ever attended. She wondered if it was the harsh reality of prison that had made Yvonne so good at focusing on the little joys in life—the gentle breeze on your face in the morning, the sight of an ant passing by your foot. Yvonne would have had very little to be grateful for within the confines of her prison cell. It was perhaps a perfect place to hone her meditation skills.

"Is this how you met?"

Marieke's expression softened. "No, we've only been together a few years. Yvonne spent over a decade working on luxury cruise ships, where she provided therapy and taught relaxation techniques to the rich and famous. Once she was in her fifties, she came to Koh Samui to start her own business. That's when we met."

"Was she already running the retreat?"

"No, that came later. When we met, she had already established a small massage studio and had dreams of starting a yoga retreat where she could offer her therapies and teach others. I, on the other hand, wanted to run a small hotel or a resort, and was looking for a location. A mutual friend thought our business ideas were similar. We joined forces, and with time, our connection deepened. We got married last year."

Harry's heart warmed at the mention of their marriage. "That's beautiful. It's clear that your hearts are rooted here on Koh Samui. I can see that it would be terrible if the news of the tragedy spread."

Marieke's eyes met Harry's. "Yes, this island holds a special place in both our hearts. It's where we found love, hope, and a new beginning. Yvonne's past may have been marked by hardship, but together, we've created a sanctuary for others to heal and find peace. If we lost this place, I don't know if we could start over again."

As the storm outside subsided, Harry thought of Yvonne and Marieke's story.

"I can see why you're so afraid, Marieke," Harry finally said. "But we can't let fear dictate our actions. James deserves justice, and the truth must come to light. We need to find a way to uncover the person responsible for his accident without endangering Yvonne."

"You're right, Harry. We can't turn a blind eye to what happened to James. If he doesn't wake up, his family will need closure. But we'll have to be careful and discreet, finding the truth without drawing attention to Yvonne's past. We owe it to James and to all those affected by this tragedy, but we can't involve the police. I don't trust them."

As their resolve grew stronger, Harry's mind raced. She knew that unraveling the truth would be a daunting task, but she also couldn't ignore the nagging sense that there might be more to the incident than met the eye. "We need to be cautious, Marieke. We can't jump to conclusions. I need time to collect my thoughts. Let's talk tomorrow."

Once Marieke left, Harry looked at her clock. It was well past two in the morning. She knew she would not be able to sleep with all the events that had taken place and the new information she had received. She needed time to process it all by herself. She went outside, stood on the wet veranda, and took several deep breaths. The air was cold and saturated with rain. The smell of soil and grass after the torrential rain was soothing and somehow reassuring. Harry found a lot of reassurance in the fact that nature persevered, no matter what.

Chapter 8

After the Storm

As Harry savored the flavors of her omelet and sipped on a refreshing banana and cinnamon smoothie, the peaceful ambiance of the restaurant allowed her to enjoy her breakfast despite the events of the previous evening. The fresh scent of the jungle, cleansed by the previous night's rain, permeated the air and brought with it a delightful earthy fragrance that entered through the restaurant's open windows. The pretty orchids in their coir baskets, now glistening with droplets of water, swayed gently in the breeze. The restaurant's large panoramic windows looked out onto the turquoise bay, its horizon merging with the blue skies, creating the illusion of infinity.

Lost in her thoughts, Harry found herself contemplating Marieke's decision not to involve the police. She understood her concerns, especially her fear of the potential consequences that might arise from a police investigation. But it left her with a sense of unease, uncertain of how to proceed. The weight of responsibility pressed upon her as she considered the precarious balance between seeking justice and protecting the innocent in a country where she had only anecdotal knowledge of the local police force's reputation.

Just as she was deep in thought, Anthony, clean-shaven and exuding an air of refined elegance, approached her table. His choice of attire reflected his impeccable taste, and Harry couldn't help but compliment his ensemble. "Anthony, you look absolutely dashing in your khaki pants and that exquisite white linen shirt with such delicate Thai embroidery! It suits you perfectly."

A modest smile graced Anthony's face as he took in the surroundings and the familiar faces scattered throughout the restaurant. He glanced across at Sarah and Euclid, engrossed in conversation, and at Mary, who was studying a local expat newspaper. With a warm and courteous demeanor, he politely asked, "May I join you, Harry? I hope I'm not interrupting your thoughts."

Harry gestured for Anthony to take a seat, eager for a friendly conversation to change her focus. "Of course, Anthony. I was just thinking about James's accident."

"That's what I wanted to talk to you about," Anthony said, placing his bowl of muesli and fresh fruit down on the table.

As Anthony leaned in closer, his voice barely above a whisper, Harry's curiosity deepened.

"I don't think it was an accident," he said, letting his words reverberate while he scooped Greek yogurt on top of his breakfast.

"Anthony, what do you mean? Are you suggesting that James's accident was intentional; that someone wanted to harm him?" Harry decided to act surprised and not reveal what she already knew.

Anthony's gaze focused on the endless horizon. "Yes, Harry. It's a theory I couldn't shake off last night as I contemplated the heated argument I overheard between Lisa and James. I wasn't deliberately eavesdropping, as you know, but the walls of these beach huts are quite thin. Sitting outside and meditating, it was impossible not to overhear."

He took a deep breath before continuing; his voice tinged with concern. "During their late-night exchange, Lisa mentioned a name: 'Helen'. She was shouting, expressing her exhaustion from competing with Helen for James's attention. It struck me as significant, as if there was more to their relationship than meets the eye."

Harry's eyes widened with surprise. "Wait, are you suggesting that James was having an affair? It doesn't seem right, Anthony. I find it hard to believe. James might not have been a perfect husband, but you know he was planning an amazing surprise for Lisa—a luxury cruise in Vietnam. I don't think a cheating husband would do that," she said in a hushed tone so as not to be overheard.

"I don't want to sound cynical, but cheating husbands can go to great lengths to keep their wives happy—to keep them unsuspecting of their secret lives."

Intrigued by Anthony's theory, Harry's mind raced with possibilities. She carefully considered his words, trying to piece together the puzzle that lay before them. Perhaps Anthony was onto something. Harry herself had never married and had never even had a serious long-term relationship. How would she know? She took a long sip of her smoothie while she considered Anthony's suggestion.

She continued. "Are you saying that Lisa may have attempted to murder her own husband?"

Anthony met her gaze. "Well, it's a serious accusation. Maybe she didn't want to kill him, but perhaps they had an argument and she hit him with whatever was lying around, like a coconut?" Anthony was cautious. "It's a possibility we cannot ignore. Considering the fights they had, the one the night before the incident, and then on the boat, coupled with his affair, it raises questions about their relationship. She might have thought it would be a perfect crime—a cheating husband killed by a falling coconut while on holiday in Thailand. I'm just saying. Being with someone for many decades is not easy. There were times in my last marriage when I felt like hitting my wife over the head with a heavy object—in the heat of the moment, I mean. I'd never act on it, of course. I'm not a psychopath, but you know what I mean... When you are with someone for many years, the stakes are high, and the emotions can take over. Our lives don't always turn out as we dreamed of when we were young. This can breed resentment towards your significant other, where we subconsciously blame *them* for our failures."

Harry's mind whirled with the implications of Anthony's words. While she couldn't question his life's experience and understanding of long-term relationships, there were still many practical questions that had to be answered. "But how could she have done it? We were all at the mindfulness session together. She was sitting not far from me."

Anthony contemplated the scenario. "That's what I've been trying to figure out most of the night. I couldn't stop thinking about it. But when you consider it carefully, the positioning of everyone's mats during the session provided a potential window of opportunity for Lisa. Her mat was situated on the edge of the group, and with everyone's eyes closed, no one would have seen her go. Also, the sound of her footsteps on the soft sand would have gone unnoticed. Lisa could have easily slipped away, carried out her attack, and returned before anyone missed her."

"Surely, Yvonne would have seen her leave the session."

"Not necessarily. If you've ever watched Yvonne during the meditation sessions, she is usually deep within herself, with her eyes closed and focused on her breathing and mantra."

Harry's eyes widened as she took in this information. The realization that anyone in their group could have left unnoticed and possibly harmed James struck her with a mix of apprehension and unease. She voiced her thoughts aloud, considering the implications.

"But Anthony, that means any one of us had the opportunity to leave momentarily, potentially inflict harm, and return without being noticed."

Anthony nodded in agreement, his eyes fixed on Harry. "Alas, the killer is one of us."

"Alas?" Harry looked at him, questioning.

"I've been reading a lot of Hercule Poirot," Anthony said, blushing momentarily. "I must have picked up some phrases."

"Anthony, are you being carried away because you've been reading Agatha Christie?" Harry whispered across the table, glad that she had not revealed what she knew about the hammer and Marieke's suspicions.

"No, Harry, I'm not imagining it. I'm sure someone tried to kill James, and it seems that anyone within our circle could have had the opportunity to carry out such an act."

"Except for Yvonne, I suppose, as we'd have noticed if she stopped the session and went away."

Their conversation was interrupted when Euclid and Sarah joined Anthony and Harry's table.

Euclid spoke first, his voice filled with concern. "It's hard to believe what happened to James. Such a terrible accident."

Sarah nodded in agreement. "I spoke to Marieke before breakfast. She looked very pale and tired. She told us the news and said that Yvonne was quite upset, too. She had to cancel today's yoga sessions."

Both Anthony and Harry expressed their understanding.

"Marieke suggested that, instead of the sessions, we take a guided tour to Wat Phra Yai, the Big Buddha temple. It's an iconic landmark here in Koh Samui."

"That sounds like a wonderful idea. Count me in." Harry felt that a day out would help her clear her head. It would also give her an opportunity to find out more about the other guests, perhaps allowing her to figure out a motive to kill James.

"What about you, Anthony?" Sarah asked. "Would you be interested in joining us on the tour?"

Anthony nodded, a faint smile appearing on his lips. "Absolutely, Sarah. I think a change of scenery might do us all some good."

As the discussion continued, Mary's voice carried across the dining room. "I'll be there too! I've always wanted to see the Big Buddha up close."

With plans agreed upon, the group decided to meet in the retreat's foyer at 11 a.m. sharp, where a minivan would transport them to the magnificent Wat Phra Yai. The prospect of exploring the temple's ornate architecture and witnessing the serenity of the beautiful golden Buddha statue offered a temporary respite from the unsettling events that had unfolded.

"Has anyone seen Amaya? Is she coming?" Harry asked.

There was silence. No one seemed to have heard from Amaya since they parted the night before.

"I'll check on her to see if she knows about the trip," Harry announced. "See you soon."

In the tranquil morning hours, as the gentle rays of sunlight pierced the lush greenery of the retreat, Harry made her way to the resort's ashram, hoping to find Amaya there. The scent of incense mingled with the subtle sounds of nature and created a serene atmosphere inside the open-air structure.

As Harry approached, she noticed Amaya seated on a cushion, lost in deep thought. Concern etched across her face, Harry softly interrupted Amaya's reverie. "Hey, Amaya. Is everything alright?"

Startled, Amaya looked up. She took a moment to collect herself before responding. "No, Harry, I'm not okay. I couldn't sleep last night. The accident... it brought back some painful memories from my childhood."

Intrigued, Harry sat down next to Amaya, offering a comforting presence. "I'm so sorry to hear that."

Amaya took a deep breath. "When I was four years old, my father died in an accident. It happened so suddenly, Harry. One moment, we were a happy family sitting around the breakfast table, making plans for the weekend. And by noon, he was gone."

Harry's heart sank, empathizing with Amaya's profound loss. "That must have been incredibly difficult for you and your family. How did you cope with such a tragedy at such a young age?"

Amaya's eyes welled up with tears as she revealed the weight she had carried for so long. "It shattered my mother, Harry. She was devastated and struggled to find her way forward in life. I didn't know it then, but she got addicted to Valium. I had to become the caregiver for my little brother, who was just two years old when it happened. I don't have many memories from my childhood, and the few I do have are quite miserable moments."

"I can imagine," Harry said, trying to comfort her friend. "You were just starting to form your conscious memories when this happened."

"I often wonder how my life would have turned out if my father hadn't died so early. Perhaps I would not be searching all the time for answers. You know, my mom never spoke about the accident. All the memories I have of him are from two blurry photos taken at a funfair."

Harry reached out, gently placing a hand on Amaya's shoulder, offering reassurance. "I can't pretend to know exactly what you've been through, but I have some idea..."

"Really?" Amaya looked at her friend, surprised to hear it.

Harry felt an unspoken connection with Amaya, as if their life experiences had woven an invisible thread between them. It was a rare occurrence for Harry to open up about her own parents, especially to someone she had just met, but something about Amaya's vulnerability and understanding compelled her to share.

"I lost my parents when I was ten years old. It was a devastating blow that made me retreat into myself during my teenage years."

"I'm so sorry, Harry. Did you have any family to take care of you?"

Harry fixed her gaze on a distant point as she continued. "I was raised by my grandparents, who I love dearly. They did their best to provide me with a stable and loving home. But there's always been a lingering void; a curiosity about what truly happened to my parents."

"What happened, Harry? If you don't mind telling me," Amaya said, her curiosity piqued.

Harry hesitated for a moment, grappling with her own emotions. She decided to tread carefully, keeping the details to herself for now. "They died in a boating accident in Koh Phangan. The day I was told about their death is still a painful memory, one that I haven't fully come to terms with. I don't know what happened exactly, but I hope to uncover the truth someday."

As the gentle scent of jasmine flowers wafted through the air inside the small ashram, Harry felt a stirring in her heart. Amaya's vulnerability had ignited her desire to open up—to share a painful memory that had lingered in the depths of her soul.

"Do you know anything about what happened?" Amaya asked.

Taking a deep breath, Harry began, her voice carrying a tinge of sadness. "I don't have any details. All I know is that they were working at the time when their boat sank, not far from here. They were both volunteering for Doctors Without Borders—I remember they'd always bring me exotic gifts from all over the world."

Amaya leaned in, her eyes filled with empathy and curiosity, encouraging Harry to continue.

"When they died, I was staying with my grandparents at the time, something I was quite accustomed to. In fact, I had my own bedroom in their house because my parents would go away for months at a time. They spent a lot of time in Malaysia, Cambodia, and Bangladesh," Harry explained, a hint of longing in her voice.

She recalled the anticipation she had felt, knowing her parents would return with stories of their adventures. But that particular trip to Thailand changed everything.

"A tourist boat from Koh Samui to Koh Phangan capsized in a violent, unexpected hurricane," Harry explained, her voice quivering with sorrow. "My parents were on board, and they drowned not far from the coast."

Harry took a deep breath, summoning the strength to recount the painful aftermath.

"A couple of weeks after the tragic news, my grandparents received my parents' ashes. They had been placed in a small urn. Together, we went to my grandmother's garden, a place filled with memories of my mom's childhood. There, next to the ancient conifer tree under which she used to play as a young girl, we scattered their ashes."

A quiet hush settled over the ashram as Amaya absorbed Harry's story. She remained silent, allowing Harry to continue at her own pace.

"For a long time, that garden became my hideaway," Harry whispered, her voice filled with nostalgia and longing. "My Grandad bought a bench with a plaque to commemorate my parents, and he set it under the tree. And my Grandma and I planted lots of daisies and marigolds around it. Whenever I missed my parents, I would sit there, feeling the gentle breeze rustle the leaves, and find comfort in the memories that lingered there. It was a way to connect with my parents; to honor their memory."

"It sounds like a lovely thing to do," Amaya said softly. "I wish I'd had a special space to commemorate my dad when I was a child. Your grandparents were very wise to have provided you that opportunity to heal."

Harry nodded. "That's true. I was fortunate to have them. Amidst the sorrow, I found comfort in their love and support. They became my pillars of strength, guiding me through the darkest of times."

Amaya's words were soft and heartfelt. "Your grandparents must be wonderful."

Harry smiled. "They truly are extraordinary. Despite their own grief, they provided unwavering love and stability. They taught me to cherish my memories and to find strength in the midst of sorrow."

"Where do they live?"

"They're still in the same old house in Ithaca. They are my biggest supporters. You know, my Grandma comments on every single post on my social media—it can be embarrassing, especially when she gets into a fight with a troll."

Amaya laughed, imagining the kind of comments a loving grandma would post on her only granddaughter's social media. In that moment, Harry and Amaya found comfort in knowing that their shared experiences forged a bond between them—a sisterhood that transcended mere words.

As the scent of incense enveloped the ashram, Harry felt renewed purpose and connection. Opening up to Amaya not only deepened their friendship but also reminded her that she was not alone on her journey toward healing and closure.

CHAPTER 9

THE BIG BUDDHA

"Ah, the frangipani's sweet scent is really strong here," Harry remarked, smiling at Amaya as they made their way toward the minivan parked outside the retreat's reception building.

"Yes, it is beautiful, but did you know that in some cultures, frangipani is considered a bad omen?"

Harry's surprise was evident. "Really? I had no idea. How can something so pretty be ominous?"

"I know. Look at this red hibiscus. It's so lovely, but in some cultures, it's considered to be the harbinger of bad luck."

Their conversation was interrupted once they reached the minivan, where Marieke and the rest of the group appeared somewhat impatient. Harry picked up on their urgency.

"Sorry. I hope you haven't been waiting too long. We're here now," Harry said, glancing at Marieke and the others. "What's going on?"

Marieke took a deep breath, addressing the entire group in a somber tone. "I was just updating everyone on what's going on with James. I've just collected Lisa from the hospital. There was no point in her staying there all night and day. She is resting in her hut. Yvonne is by her side, awaiting any news from the hospital. At the moment, James's condition is stable, but the doctors are considering whether to transport him to a better-equipped hospital in Bangkok."

Harry's heart sank at the news. "Is there anything we can do to help? Anything at all?"

Marieke offered a faint smile. "Right now, all we can do is support them with our presence and keep them in our thoughts. Lisa's daughter will arrive tomorrow evening, but unfortunately her son won't be able to make it. He's in the middle of his exams, but he'll join his mom and sister as soon as he finishes them."

The severity of the situation hung in the air as the group absorbed the information. They were reminded of the fragility of life and the importance of cherishing every moment. As they boarded the minivan, their anticipation was mixed with concern. The trip should prove a welcome distraction amidst the swirling turmoil of their emotions.

Inside the van, Marieke, despite her exhaustion and stress, summoned a brave smile and an optimistic tone. She understood the importance of keeping spirits lifted in such challenging times.

"Let's stay positive, everyone," Marieke said, her voice filled with determination. "James is in good hands, and the Thai doctors are doing everything they can to ensure his recovery. Once we're given permission, I'll arrange a visit to the hospital so we can show him our support."

Her words brought a glimmer of hope to the group as they listened attentively, grateful for Marieke's strength in the face of adversity.

As the minivan made its way toward Wat Phra Yai, Marieke shifted the group's focus to their upcoming destination. She shared some touristy information, adopting a tone similar to that of a tour guide. Her determination to keep her remaining guests happy was evident.

"So let me tell you a little bit about Wat Phra Yai, also known as the Big Buddha temple. It is one of the most famous landmarks on Koh Samui, and it features a magnificent statue of Buddha that stands at an impressive 12 meters tall. The statue is adorned in golden robes and is a symbol of peace and serenity," Marieke explained.

She continued sharing interesting tidbits about the temple's history, architectural details, and cultural significance.

"As we explore the temple grounds, you'll have the opportunity to appreciate the intricate design of the temple's structures, admire the stunning views from the hilltop location, and learn about the customs and traditions associated with Thai Buddhism. Afterwards, we can visit the nearby Fisherman's Village, known for its charming streets lined with traditional wooden houses, market stalls, and delicious local cuisine."

"Do you think we could have lunch in Fisherman's Village?" Mary asked. "I've heard wonderful things about the restaurants there."

"Of course. I'll take you to my favorite place."

Marieke's enthusiasm and informative talk infused the atmosphere with a sense of adventure and cultural discovery. The group began to immerse themselves in the journey, momentarily forgetting their worries as they became enchanted by the allure of Koh Samui's rich heritage.

As soon as they parked the van and got out of the vehicle, they could see the majestic golden statue. It towered over the temple grounds, emanating a sense of power and spiritual significance. The sunlight reflected off its gilded surface, casting a radiant glow that seemed to shimmer across the entire area.

Euclid's curious gaze focused on a group of locals nearby, who were reverently burning incense sticks and offering prayers. Intrigued, he turned to Marieke and asked, "What are they doing with the incense? Is it a religious ritual?"

Marieke nodded. "Yes, it's a traditional Thai Buddhist ritual," she explained. "Burning incense is a way of paying respect and making offerings to the Buddha. It symbolizes purification, enlightenment, and the dissemination of positive energy."

Mary, always interested in topics of spiritual enlightenment and religion, joined the conversation. "I've been wondering about the difference between Thai Buddhism and Indian Buddhism. Have you got any idea, Marieke?"

Marieke took a moment to reflect before responding. "Well, I'm not an expert. From what I understand, both Thai and Indian Buddhism share a common foundation in the teachings of the Buddha, but there are some distinct cultural and ritualistic differences," she explained. "In Thailand, there is a strong emphasis on spirit worship and the incorporation of local beliefs into Buddhist practices. We also have unique traditions, such as the Wai Khru ceremony, where students pay respect to their teachers, and the Loi Krathong festival, where we release floating lanterns on the water to symbolize letting go of negativity."

"That's so interesting," Sarah chimed in. "I'd like to see these festivals."

Mary nodded pensively. "What about Korea? Are the rituals there similar to those here?" she asked.

Sarah hesitated for a moment, then admitted, "To be honest, my knowledge of Buddhism is quite superficial. My parents are Mormons, and I grew up in that church. But I can tell you that Buddhism in Korea has its own distinct practices and rituals influenced by Korean culture and traditions. There are beautiful temples, meditation practices, and important festivals like the Buddha's Birthday, which is celebrated with lantern parades. It's kind of similar to Thailand but also very different, if that makes sens e."

As Sarah and Mary continued their conversation about the intersections of religion, culture, and personal experience, Marieke stepped aside and let everyone explore the temple grounds at their own pace.

"I need to speak to you in private," she whispered to Harry as she walked past. "Follow me, please."

Harry followed her away from the other guests. Once out of earshot, Harry locked eyes with Marieke, intrigued by her secretive tone and demeanor.

Taking a quick glance around to ensure that their conversation remained private, Marieke began, "Harry, this morning, I discreetly spoke to each of my staff members, hoping to uncover any information that could help us. I asked them if they had seen anyone behaving in a suspicious way or anything out of the ordinary."

"Good idea," Harry said, nodding. "Did you find anything?"

"Yes, I did. During my conversation with the chef, she mentioned something that caught my attention."

Harry listened intently. The thought that a potential lead had been discovered sent a surge of adrenaline through her veins.

"She reported that while she was disposing of the kitchen rubbish during the evening mindfulness session, she saw someone running toward the beach," Marieke continued. "She thought it was strange because the figure was covered by a black sarong."

"What do you mean?"

"The head and the face were hidden under the sarong—as if the person did not want to be seen. All the chef saw were dark yoga pants—just like the ones we hand out to our guests when they arrive at the retreat. The chef is sure it was a guest but she can't be certain which one."

Harry's mind raced, attempting to piece together the fragments of information they had gathered so far. The image of a dark figure fleeing toward the beach during the yoga session painted a mysterious and potentially significant picture.

"Could she guess whether it was a man or a woman?" Harry asked, her voice barely audible above the ambient sounds of the temple.

"Not really. She saw the figure from some distance and against the setting sun. It could be anyone."

"Is she sure it was one of the guests?"

"As sure as one can be," Marieke reflected. "I think she assumed it was one of the guests because of the clothes."

"If she only saw the back, it might as well have been a man concealing his identity under the sarong." Harry was not convinced that this was the case, but wanted to leave all the logical possibilities open. Whoever hit James on the head had to be physically strong.

"You make a good point. What's important is that it confirms our suspicion that there's someone out there who tried to kill James. We need to continue our inquiries discreetly." Marieke gave Harry an earnest look. "We'll find out who this person is and what he or she was doing there. Together, we'll get to the bottom of this."

"Yes, I agree that we have to tread gently. We don't want this person to know we are on their trail. Let's not share this with anyone else."

Chapter 10

Fishermen's Village

The group had left the Buddha temple and were seated at a large, rustic wooden table in a bustling seafood restaurant in the heart of Fishermen's Village. The air was filled with the lively buzz of conversation, laughter, and the tantalizing aroma of grilled fish and fragrant Thai spices that wafted from the open kitchen. Colorful lanterns adorned the ceiling.

As the group chatted animatedly, sharing stories of their travels, a friendly waitress approached their table. Dressed in a traditional Thai outfit, she exuded a sense of gracious warmth and hospitality.

"Sawadee-ka," she said, bowing slightly and with her palms pressed together. "Welcome to *Thai Tide*. May I recommend some of our specialties from Fishermen's Village?"

"That would be wonderful," Mary said on everyone's behalf.

"Our grilled tiger prawns are marinated in fresh ginger, garlic, and chilies. They're succulent and full of flavor. I also recommend our guests' favorite dish: the traditional fish curry. It consists of fish in a rich coconut broth with aromatic herbs and spices. And for those who enjoy spicy dishes, our fiery basil chili squid is not to be missed."

"What's the catch of the day?" Marieke, who was familiar with the restaurant's menu, asked.

"It's sea bass," the waitress informed her. "It's steamed and served with lime and chilies. It's to die for."

Marieke, sensing that the group would have a hard time choosing, asked them if they'd like to share a selection of the dishes that the waitress had just recommended. They all agreed.

"I'd suggest some of our pineapple fried rice to share, too," the waitress said as she was writing down the order. "It's served in a pineapple shell, and it's a great complement to the spicy seafood."

"Sound wonderful. We'll try that too," Marieke said.

"Could you recommend a wine to go with the seafood?" Anthony asked, while putting down the menu.

"My favorite for what you've just ordered would be Riesling. It's white and slightly sweet. It goes so well with Thai food."

The group agreed to order a couple of bottles for the table.

"Excellent choices. I'll be right back with your wine," she assured them before disappearing into the bustling kitchen.

As they awaited their food, toasts were made to their adventures, and Euclid thanked Marieke for organizing this wonderful trip. The clinking of glasses harmonized with the lively atmosphere of the restaurant, creating a symphony of laughter, conversation, and the occasional burst of excited chatter from nearby tables.

Anthony, taking a sip of Riesling, couldn't help but express his satisfaction. "This wine is exceptional; it will go perfectly with the flavors of the sea bass. The acidity is just right," he remarked, nodding approvingly.

Soon, the sharing plates of various fish and seafood dishes started to appear in front of them. They were all beautifully presented in a way that ensured everyone could have a small helping.

Mary's taste buds danced with joy. "OMG! This basil chili squid! The balance of spice and herbs is absolutely divine. Although it's a bit hot," she said while waving her hand in front of her open mouth in an attempt to cool it down.

"Mary, not again," Anthony said, laughing at her amiably. "Why do you insist on eating spicy food?"

"I really like it," Mary said, struggling now to speak. "But it doesn't like me." Her eyes started to water as she tried to take deep breaths with her mouth open. Harry found it hard not to smile at Mary's antics.

"I'll get you some sliced cucumber or yogurt," Marieke said as she walked away in the direction of the kitchen.

"I think I'll lay off chilies for a while," Mary informed the table once she recovered, somewhat embarrassed about causing another chili incident.

As the compliments for the dishes echoed around the table, Mary's face fell, clouded by remorse. "I feel guilty for enjoying this meal and the wine while James is in a coma and Lisa is alone in her hut at the retreat," she confessed.

Marieke gave Mary a reassuring smile. "Don't blame yourself. Yvonne is with Lisa, offering support and care during this difficult time. We all need this moment to gather our thoughts and recharge so we can be there for Lisa if worse comes to worst," she assured, her voice filled with empathy.

Anthony, refilling everyone's wine glasses, seemed momentarily to exhibit a hint of aloofness. His gaze fixed on the golden liquid. "Let's not dwell on the sadness," he suggested. "We're here to support each other, and part of that means taking moments of respite amidst the chaos."

Amaya, understanding the need for emotional distance, spoke up, her voice gentle yet resolute. "Mary, it's important to give ourselves permission to enjoy moments like these. By taking care of ourselves, we can gather strength to face whatever lies ahead."

Harry, nodding in agreement with Amaya's words, offered her support as well. "You're right, Amaya. We must find the strength within ourselves at this challenging time. Together, we can support Lisa and each other with friendship," she said, her voice filled with determination.

As the conversation shifted to exploring other captivating places to visit in Thailand, the group eagerly shared their recommendations. While the chatter about tourist attractions filled the air, Harry's mind drifted to darker thoughts. Her gaze lingered on her companions, quietly assessing each one. She contemplated the possibilities, considering the motives that could have driven someone in their midst to commit such a heinous act.

Both Amaya and Sarah owned a selection of sarongs. Harry had seen them wearing sarongs on the beach at the retreat. Amaya had an unresolved trauma from her childhood. Could James have been involved? Was he the driver of the car that killed Amaya's father? But Harry quickly dismissed this scenario. The notion that Amaya would travel to another continent to confront her father's killer seemed very far-fetched.

Sarah, on the other hand, remained somewhat of an enigma to Harry. There was a lack of depth in Harry's understanding of her motives. Had James wronged her in some way, leading her to seek revenge? The possibilities lingered, but Harry found it difficult to piece the puzzle together.

Her attention then turned to Mary; a chatterbox with a seemingly endless supply of anecdotes and entertainment. But upon closer reflection, Harry realized that she didn't know much about Mary's personal life. Yet, Harry couldn't ignore the fact that Mary had been the one who saved James's life after the incident. It seemed contradictory for someone with ill intentions to act heroically in the face of an emergency.

As Harry observed the three cheerful women, laughter and camaraderie filled the air. She struggled to find a motive that would implicate any of them in the attempted murder. Doubt crept into her mind. Could it have been an accident, a twist of Fate that had taken a dark turn? A heated argument that had gone out of control? Harry's mind was awash with unanswered questions, the mystery deepening with each passing moment. Was it Lisa? Could it have been her silhouette that the cook saw against the setting sun? And who was the Helen that Anthony had mentioned before? Harry made a mental note of these questions.

Her ruminations were interrupted when Sarah inquired about the arrival of Lisa and James's daughter.

"Clara will be here tomorrow evening. Thank you, Sarah. I truly appreciate your offer to look after her," Marieke replied.

"Perhaps Lisa's daughter can tell us who Helen is?" Anthony looked at Harry from across the table as if he had been reading her mind all along.

"Helen?" Mary asked.

"Oh, it's nothing," Anthony said, waving it away. "Just something that has been bothering me. I'm sure it will become clear soon."

The atmosphere at the table shifted as Marieke raised her glass, seeking the attention of her companions. "I want to thank each and every one of you for being so supportive during this difficult time. When Yvonne and I opened this retreat a few years ago, we never could have imagined that something as tragic as this would ever occur."

A collective sense of empathy filled the air as Marieke continued, "This place was meant to be a sanctuary—a haven of happiness and healing. And while I felt defeated and lost last night, your understanding and compassion have given me strength." Her voice wavered with emotion, but a glimmer of hope shone through her words.

The group, sensing Marieke's vulnerability, rallied around her. Glasses clinked together in a toast as they raised them high, offering words of encouragement and support. "We're here for you, Marieke," Harry said, her voice filled with sincerity. The others joined in, echoing their sentiments and reassuring Marieke that they would stand by her side throughout this ordeal.

Chapter 11

On the Jetty

It was late at night, and Lamai had just finished preparing her boat for the next day. The playful moonlight danced upon the mirrored surface of Koh Samui's bay. The glow of the moon cast an ethereal radiance, illuminating the scene with a cool metallic allure. The jetty, a bustling hub during the day, now lay still and deserted, its empty wooden planks extending over the calm waters.

Several small boats and fishing vessels were moored to the jetty, their hulls swaying almost imperceptibly with the gentle lapping of the waves. Some modern jet skis, also dormant for the night, rested nearby, their garish colors muted in the darkened surroundings. The rhythmic chorus of night birds and insects in the jungle beyond created a soothing background symphony, blending seamlessly with the whispers of the sea.

Lamai lay alone on the sandy beach next to the jetty. This was her moment of respite from the demanding role she held as a captain of a tour boat. As she lay motionless, her mind drifted into introspection. She reflected upon her life journey that had brought her to this quiet part of the world.

She recalled the laborious days her grandmother and mother spent toiling in the rice fields; their dedication to achieving something more than mere subsistence was etched deep within her soul. She pictured the sun-soaked vistas of Isaan, where countless women like her family members would gather to collect the harvest. She had a deep respect for agricultural work, but had wanted a different life for herself. That's why she joined the Naval Academy and trained to be a captain.

Her love for her family roots and the tireless efforts of those who came before her filled Lamai with a sense of relief and deep gratitude. She recognized the progress she had made by gaining her maritime qualifications and securing her own boat. Now, she worked with tourists from all walks of life. Although the long hours and occasional encounters with demanding individuals could test her patience, Lamai found a sense of self-worth, knowing that she was forging a better future for herself.

As Lamai gazed up at the celestial tapestry above, she marveled at the stars punctuating the vast expanse of the night sky. In their shimmering brilliance, she found inspiration and a reminder of the infinite possibilities that awaited her on this island of dreams. In her mind's eye, she saw two perfect little children: a boy and a girl. Her own children one day? They'd live in a beautiful villa on Samui. By then, she would not have to work on her own boat. She'd own several tour boats and manage them from an office on land. In the evenings, she'd cook delicious sticky rice and meat for her family, and they'd sit on the veranda until late at night, listening to the jungle and making plans for the future.

Lamai's daydreaming came to an abrupt halt as the sound of footsteps reverberated across the wooden planks of the jetty. The creaking timbers alerted her senses, and she instinctively glanced up, her eyes piercing through the darkness. Emerging from the shadows, a figure moved with hurried stealth, clad in a long black cloak that billowed in the night breeze. A dark scarf concealed the person's features, making identification a challenge.

Intrigued by the mysterious presence, Lamai's curiosity compelled her to observe the unfolding scene. From her recumbent position, her gaze fixed upon the figure as it swiftly made its way to the edge of the jetty, holding tightly onto a bag. She could not clearly see what was inside, but it appeared to be heavy.

The silhouette took a dark object out of the bag and cast it into the depths of the sea when they heard Lamai's friendly "Hello!" from the beach. Startled, the figure jumped and turned towards the beach. Lamai's eyes widened in recognition, for she suddenly realized the identity of the cloaked figure before her. Lamai found it hard to understand what the person was doing on the jetty so late at night and what was thrown into the sea.

But it was too late. Unbeknownst to Lamai, this seemingly innocent greeting would seal her fate. The figure, previously oblivious to Lamai's presence and the impending danger she posed, pivoted in response to the friendly voice. The cloak swirled around its form, momentarily obscuring the face from view.

"Hello, Captain Lamai," the voice responded. "I was just looking for you. Do you have a minute?"

CHAPTER 12

THE DISAPPEARANCE

As the early morning sun began to paint the sky with pink and gold, Harry lay on her bed in her thatched hut, her mind consumed by the fragments of the mysterious jigsaw occupying her thoughts. The rhythmic beat of the sea's waves reached her through the open window and provided a comforting backdrop to her contemplations. Frustration gnawed at her as the pieces of the puzzle refused to fit together, leaving her yearning for more information about the guests at the retreat.

Suddenly, a resounding knock on the door broke her tranquil stillness, jolting Harry from her speculations. The hour was early, but her curiosity was mingled with concern as Anthony's voice seeped through the closed door, inquiring whether she was awake.

"I am now," she assured him as she swung the door open to reveal a weary and troubled Anthony. Apologizing for the untimely intrusion, he confessed to having spent another sleepless night.

"I need to talk things over," he confessed. "There are just so many elements to James's mysterious accident. I feel two heads will be better than one when trying to figure it out. Would you mind being my sounding board?"

It was clear Anthony needed someone with whom he could dissect the events that had unfolded. She could not help but admit to sharing his frustration. Harry gestured to the rattan armchairs on the veranda.

There, they sat in silent companionship for some moments, allowing the gentle glow of the rising sun to warm their faces as it painted the world in a delicate pastel palette.

"So, have you got any idea for a motive? Any suspects?" Harry asked, opening the conversation.

"To be frank, I can see plenty of motives," Anthony said quite earnestly. "As I told you and Mary before, I find James and his type, 'financial advisors', quite despicable. They gamble with other people's money and never take any responsibility, but..."

Harry nodded empathically to show her understanding. Moved by Anthony's quest to find the killer, Harry decided to disclose what she had gleaned thus far, except for the bloodied hammer.

"The chef saw a figure clad in a dark sarong and yoga pants running towards the beach during the meditation session," Harry said, sharing the new information that their prime suspect might be a woman.

She hoped to invite a collaborative brainstorming session, during which they could weave together the fragments of their knowledge to create a more comprehensive account of James's accident. As the morning sun warmed the veranda, Harry stretched on the armchair and looked up at the coconut palm tree leaves swaying in the breeze.

"Do you think it was Helen, the mystery woman?" Anthony pondered the situation and looked at Harry. "I feel like I should talk to Lisa and find out once and for all who this Helen is."

Harry scratched her head. "Honestly, I don't think that's a good idea," she replied. "We need to tread carefully. Lisa is already going through a lot, and approaching her directly might not yield the answers we're looking for."

"But don't you think it's possible that Lisa could be responsible for James's condition?" Anthony pressed, wanting to explore every possibility.

"That's even more reason why we should not discuss it with her directly, I feel. We still don't know much about this family."

"You're right," Anthony admitted. "Secrets can run deep, you know? I've seen families that seemed perfect on the surface but had many skeletons in their closet. But I find the whole mystery very frustrating."

Harry nodded, understanding his point. "I'm with you, but jumping to conclusions without concrete evidence won't help. I think it would be better if we gather more information first. We really need to know more about James, Lisa, and the other guests. We should not eliminate anyone."

"What if James had a hidden life, like a second wife or another family?" Anthony suggested. "What if Lisa found out about it?"

Harry paused, considering the idea. "It's a possibility," she admitted. "But I believe it might be more helpful to speak with Clara when she gets here. She may have a clearer understanding of the family dynamics and any hidden truths."

Anthony approved. "That's a good idea. Clara might provide valuable insight into their relationship. I'll keep an eye out for her arrival."

"Agreed," Harry replied. "Let's not jump to any conclusions about Lisa just yet. Now, let's consider the other 'suspects'."

"What about Marieke? We haven't considered her yet. She does match the description. We shouldn't rule her out..." Anthony was deep in thought.

Harry leaned back in her armchair, contemplating whether to tell Anthony about the hammer that Marieke had found, but once again decided to keep her cards close to her chest. It didn't make sense to Harry that Marieke would involve herself in the investigation if she were the culprit. *She would have covered her tracks better. She wouldn't have brought the possibility of foul play to my attention.*

"Marieke doesn't seem like a likely suspect," Harry said after a short reflection. "If James dies, she's going to lose her business. I don't see the motive."

"You're quite right. If Marieke were guilty, she wouldn't have told you about the suspicious figure either. It just doesn't add up. I think we can exclude her and Yvonne. They have too much to lose."

They both fell into a contemplative silence, their thoughts swirling with unanswered questions. After a moment, Harry spoke up hesitantly. "I know this might sound far-fetched, but what if the figure the cook saw was a man hiding under a large sarong?"

Anthony raised an eyebrow. "What are you suggesting?"

"Well, we haven't considered Euclid," Harry replied. "We can't dismiss any possibilities. Also, he wasn't at the mindfulness session. He only showed up when he heard the commotion, and then Mary asked him to help with the CPR. Apparently, he was taking a nap in his hut."

Anthony rolled his eyes, clearly skeptical. "Now you're just guessing, Harry. Euclid is an African American man. I'm sure the cook would have mentioned that if she had seen him. She'd spot the color of his hands or feet. It would stand out."

Harry sighed, acknowledging the weakness of her suggestion. "You're right, it's a long shot. But we have to keep our minds open. We can't afford to overlook anything, even if it seems unlikely. Sometimes clues can be deceiving, and coincidences can play tricks on us ."

Anthony's expression was thoughtful. "I suppose you're right. We shouldn't close ourselves off to any line of inquiry. Let's continue to explore every possibility. I'll try to find out more about Euclid. I didn't remember that he wasn't with us at the mindfulness session."

Harry looked at her watch. "Shall we have breakfast? They're about to open the restaurant."

"That's a great idea. Let's go."

As Harry and Anthony approached the main reception area together, they noticed a visibly distressed man engaged in a tense conversation with Marieke. Harry's curiosity deepened, and she exchanged a concerned look with Anthony, silently agreeing to find out what had upset the man.

Their intentions were helped when Marieke beckoned them closer, her voice laced with worry. "Harry, Anthony, this is Preecha, one of Captain Lamai's crew," she explained, her tone tinged with apprehension.

Before Marieke could elaborate, Preecha interjected in a hurried manner, speaking rapidly in Thai. His intense agitation was palpable, and Marieke attempted to calm him down.

"Preecha has been trying to reach Captain Lamai since early this morning," Marieke relayed, her voice filled with concern. "She hasn't been answering her phone, and that's highly unusual. The crew is usually on the boat at 6 a.m. to prepare for the day. Preecha said he then discovered Lamai's phone lying near the jetty."

A wave of unease washed over Harry. The missing captain raised alarming possibilities, and a sense of urgency gripped her.

"We need to take action. We should contact the authorities and report this immediately," Anthony declared, his voice resolute.

Anthony's belief that it was imperative they involve the police was fervently supported by Preecha in broken English. Harry, understanding why Marieke didn't want the police presence at the retreat, exchanged a knowing glance with her, silently assuring her that their shared secret would remain intact.

"Perhaps we should drive to Lamai's house to see if she's there," Harry said, proposing an alternate course of action. "It's possible that she misplaced her phone on her way home last night. She might still be sleeping there soundly."

Marieke grasped the significance of Harry's suggestion and translated it to Preecha, who initially looked somewhat perplexed but then agreed with Harry's idea. Perhaps the Captain's lost phone served as her alarm clock. He hoped it to be true. They all followed Marieke to where her car was parked near the reception area.

They drove along the tree-lined roadway toward Lamai's house in silence, the car's engine echoing through the quiet morning air. Harry couldn't help but wonder what they would find. *Was Lamai safe inside, oblivious to the turmoil her absence had caused? Or would their search reveal a more sinister truth?*

The traditional wooden stilt house stood proudly amidst its lush background, its elevated structure offering glimpses of the tropical paradise behind the house. Well-tended, majestic mango trees swayed gently in the morning breeze, their bountiful fruits hanging temptingly from their branches. The cultivated greenery formed a homely backdrop, enhancing the beauty of the rustic setting. The presence of chickens and two small piglets added a touch of liveliness to the scene. These domestic animals scurried around beneath the house, looking for scraps of food and the occasional insect.

Marieke parked the car on the grass outside the house. It was still early, but she raised her voice as she called out to see if anyone was present.

"Lamai lives here with her grandmother, who came to Samui a few years ago to retire from the rice fields and to help her granddaughter," Marieke said, explaining the farm setting to Harry and Anthony. "Her family is originally from the north, the 'rice bowl' of Thailand, as it's called."

As they approached the house, an elderly Thai woman emerged from an outbuilding. She was clearly in the middle of some farmwork. Her weathered face reflected a life rich with experience. Dressed in a loose-fitting shirt and cotton pants, she wore a traditional farmer's hat that protected her whole face from the sun. The woman moved swiftly as she approached the visitors.

As soon as she recognized Preecha, they started to speak in Thai. It was clear from their body language that Preecha was asking her about the captain's whereabouts. The atmosphere grew tense as Marieke translated the conversation between Lamai's grandmother and Preecha. The worry etched on the grandmother's face was unmistakable, and her concern for Lamai was evident, even if one did not understand the language. The repetition of Lamai's name during the exchange sent a shiver down Harry's spine.

Before Marieke could even translate, Harry had already gathered the general meaning of the conversation. Lamai hadn't returned home, and her absence was raising alarms. Marieke's translation confirmed that Lamai had called the previous evening, explaining that she had a heavy workload and had to stay late. The grandmother thought that Lamai had decided to sleep on the boat. She did it sometimes instead of riding her scooter late at night.

Preecha turned to Marieke and spoke in English, "We need to call the police! Lamai is not on the boat!"

Harry silently agreed with Preecha's assessment of the situation. She hoped Marieke would change her mind about involving the police and she wasn't disappointed.

Marieke's voice was filled with worry as she replied, "You're right, Preecha. We have to contact the police immediately."

Preecha's hand shook as he held his phone, dialing the number that would bring the authorities into the unfolding events. Anticipation hung in the air, and the garden in which they stood was filled with silence.

Harry couldn't help but voice her concern. "I hope Captain Lamai is safe."

"We'll do everything we can, Harry. Hopefully, the police will be able to locate her. I hope that there is some kind of misunderstanding. Maybe she forgot to tell everyone where she was going?" Marieke said, but Harry found it hard to believe that an adult, hard-working woman would abandon her job and family and disappear.

As the call connected, the group fell into an anxious silence, broken only by the muffled conversation on the phone.

"The police will meet us at the jetty," Preecha said, hanging up the phone and informing everyone.

He then spoke to the grandmother, who had tears rolling down her paper-thin cheeks. The wise woman clearly thought something terrible must have happened to her only granddaughter.

Chapter 13

BLACK SARONG

Harry and Anthony stood on the beach outside the yoga retreat, their gazes fixed on the jetty where several Thai police officers were speaking with the crew of Lamai's boat. The air was tense as they waited for any updates.

Anthony broke the silence, his voice filled with concern. "Do you think Lamai's disappearance is somehow connected to James's accident, Harry?"

Harry considered the question. "It's hard to say, Anthony. During the boat trip, I noticed James talking to the captain quite a bit. Perhaps he shared something with her that could lead us to the person who tried to harm him."

Anthony nodded, his eyes searching for answers. "That's what I was thinking, too. But when I saw them talking together, what they were discussing seemed inconsequential. Just casual conversation about the island and the weather. I didn't catch anything that could have triggered such a violent act."

Frustration tinged Harry's voice as she replied, "I agree, Anthony. It feels like we have all the pieces of the puzzle, but they don't quite fit together. And now, with the captain's sudden disappearance, it only adds another layer of mystery. I'm struggling to link her and James. We're missing a crucial detail. Something or someone that would join both cases."

Anthony's gaze shifted toward Marieke, who was approaching the police officers. "I'll go and see if they found any clues on the boat," he said, determination evident in his voice. "Maybe they've discovered something that could shed light on this whole situation."

"Please do," Harry urged, her eyes following Anthony's retreating figure. "We need any information we can get. Lamai might hold the key to unraveling this mystery. Just be cautious, Anthony. We don't know who we can trust at this point. And..." Harry hesitated but felt obliged to say what was on her mind. "Let's not mention our suspicions about James's accident to the police. It's best at this stage not to set off the alarm bells."

Naturally distrustful of any authorities, Anthony conceded without asking for clarification. As he made his way toward Marieke and the police officers, Harry remained on the beach, lost in her thoughts. The weight of the unknown pressed on her. She scanned the place, hoping to find a clue that would bring them closer to the truth. Time was slipping away, and with the captain gone, the pressure to find out what was going on couldn't have been greater.

As Harry walked along the beach, she reached the edge of the mangroves that dotted parts of the shoreline of Koh Samui. The tall, slender trees with their distinctive stilt-like roots provided a natural habitat for a multitude of creatures. The air was thick with the scent of saltwater and the earthy fragrance of mangrove mud. Harry could hear the calls of a white-bellied sea eagle soaring above, and she spotted a group of colorful kingfishers darting between the branches as they searched for the tiny fish that dwelt in the shallow mangrove waters. She took a few deep breaths and, despite the tragic events, felt grateful for being in these stunning surroundings.

Lost in her thoughts, Harry pondered Marieke's decision not to involve the police in James's case. If the captain's disappearance was deemed suspicious, they would want to interview the guests who were on the boat a few days ago. They might even want to search the retreat. She wondered if Marieke had used the time they had when they returned from Lamai's house to warn people about the potential investigation. Had Marieke spoken to Yvonne about the situation? Harry had seen neither Yvonne nor Lisa since the accident, having been unsure if she was emotionally ready to face the woman whose husband was fighting for his life.

Her mind drifted back to her own childhood, remembering the tragic boating accident that took her parents' lives. She had been far away, shielded from the immediate horror of the event. The reality of their permanent absence had taken time to sink in; weeks spent in futile hope that they would return. The pain and grief of losing someone dear was immeasurable, and Harry empathized with Lisa's unimaginable anguish.

Suddenly, her reflections were interrupted by a peculiar sight among the exposed mangroves. At first, a sense of fear gripped Harry as she mistook the object for a massive snake lurking in the shallows. Startled, she stumbled back, splashing clumsily into the shallow waters. But as her heart rate slowed and her eyes adjusted to the gloom underneath the trees, she realized that what she was looking at was a large piece of black fabric tangled amidst the mangrove roots.

Curiosity getting the better of her, Harry approached the tangled fabric and gingerly removed it from the muddy vegetation. It revealed itself to be a black sarong, its silky texture contrasting against the rough backdrop of the mangroves. She couldn't help but wonder how it had ended up there and whether it held any significance to the ongoing investigation.

With the sarong in hand, Harry's mind buzzed with questions. Who did it belong to? How did it find its way into the mangroves? Was it a clue or merely a thoughtlessly discarded item? She raised the fabric up so she could view the whole garment. As her fingers traced the intricate black embroidery along its edges, a flicker of recognition sparked in her mind. She had seen this pattern before. It was unmistakably the same pattern that Amaya had worn on the boat trip. Sinister questions swirled through Harry's mind, intertwined with a growing sense of unease. Why had Amaya's sarong been left abandoned near Lamai's boat? Was Amaya not who she claimed to be?

Realizing the importance of her discovery, Harry made up her mind to hand over the sarong to the police officers who were leaving Captain Lamai's boat. She quickened her pace, calling out to get their attention. "Excuse me! Excuse me!" Marieke, trailing behind the officers, turned to face Harry with surprise in her eyes. Overcome by the seriousness of her finding, Harry requested Marieke's assistance in explaining what she had found to the officers.

Marieke translated Harry's words while Harry extended the sarong toward them, hoping to convey the significance of her find. However, the officers regarded her with a mix of indifference and skepticism, their attention swiftly shifting away from her to the notes that they had taken in their police pocketbooks. They walked away, seemingly dismissing Harry and her discovery as inconsequential.

A wave of frustration washed over Harry, but she refused to be deterred. She was convinced that the sarong held important clues, and she couldn't let the trivializing response of the officers discourage her pursuit of the truth. Determined to uncover the connection between Amaya, James, and Lamai, Harry resolved to keep the sarong and delve deeper into the mystery on her own.

As the police car drove off, Harry couldn't help but feel a wave of dissatisfaction. She turned to Marieke, her voice tinged with frustration, and asked, "What did the police say?"

Marieke sighed. "They said the sarong could belong to anyone. According to them, there are plenty of lost items on the beach, so they don't consider it significant."

Anthony's concern was evident, "But did they find any clues on Lamai's boat? Anything that could help locate her?"

Marieke shook her head, disappointed. "They didn't tell me much. You know... Thai police are very formal. They do not like to cooperate with civilians or share any of their findings. But the little I know is that there was no sign of struggle or forced entry into the sleeping cabin. Since Captain Lamai is an adult, the police dismissed it as a simple case of her merely going away without informing anyone. They told the crew to contact them if she doesn't return within a few days, but they won't start a missing person search yet."

Anthony's disquiet was palpable. "This is outrageous! We can't just wait around while Captain Lamai is missing! She's a responsible adult, a captain; she would never disappear without telling her crew or her grandmother."

Harry nodded in agreement. "I agree, Anthony. I only met her once, but she did not strike me as an airhead. Assuming that she has gone away makes no sense. We need to do something. We can't let this go unresolved." She turned to Marieke, determination in her eyes. "I'm going to keep the sarong. It may be a crucial clue, and I want to keep it safe in case the police change their mind."

Harry pulled a plastic bag from her satchel, carefully placing the sarong inside it and securing the two hand loops with a loose knot. "For now, I'll hold on to it. I don't know exactly what it means yet, but I'm certain it's connected to both James's case and Lamai's disappearance. I'll dry it and then try to find its owner."

Marieke nodded. "That's a good idea, Harry. We need to find answers, and if the police don't take it seriously, we'll have to uncover the truth ourselves."

Chapter 14

The Tide

Captain Lamai's eyes struggled to adjust to the darkness that enveloped the cave walls surrounding her. She could hear the distant crashing of waves, a rhythmic reminder of the sea's presence. Disoriented, she attempted to sit up from the damp, hard ground, but her body felt heavy and sluggish. A slow panic began to rise within her as she realized her hands were bound tightly behind her back.

The stench of guano and stagnant sea water filled her nostrils, causing a sickening sensation in her stomach. Lamai's mind raced, desperately trying to piece together her surroundings. She knew this cave was accessible only during low tide, and otherwise remained concealed from the world. Fear gripped her as she understood the dire situation she was in.

Struggling to collect her thoughts, Lamai fought against the constraints that held her captive. She could feel the wet sandy rocks beneath her body, evidence of the receding tide. With a racing mind, she calculated that she had thirteen hours until the cave would be completely submerged by the next high tide. She knew that at night, the waters would rise to a spring tide level, increasing the depth of the water that would rush into the cave.

Her heart pounded in her chest as she tried to recall how she had ended up in this treacherous predicament, but her mind was blank. But there was no time to dwell on how she got here. Sensing that her feet were bound, too, she took a second to compose herself. "I must find a way out," Lamai whispered. She began to calm herself as she recalled the many hours of endurance training in cold water that she went through at the Naval Academy. The rigors of her training proved that she had stamina. She steeled her will to survive with fortitude and experience. She was going to get out of there. But first, she had to make sure she didn't drown at the next high tide.

Examining her bound feet, she knew she had to reach to a spot higher up in the cave, away from the encroaching water. Each inching movement she took was painstakingly slow, every tiny shift of her body a struggle against time. Lamai knew she had to persevere, summoning every ounce of strength to worm her way from the impending watery grave that awaited her. In her mind's eye, she was back at the Naval Academy. It was just another exercise in self-control and preservation. Her old endurance instructor was standing over her, shouting commands.

In the gloom of the cave, Lamai fought valiantly against her restraints, her mind consumed with survival. Her race against time had begun, and she was determined to defy the odds and emerge from the depths of this rancid cave, propelled by her desire for freedom. Inch by inch, she squirmed painfully toward the sharp limestone rocks that lined the back of the cave.

Chapter 15

At the Beach Bar

Rosie's Shipwreck, a quirky beach bar built inside an open cave in the rocky part of the shore, exuded a charming ambiance with lanterns hanging over the bar and many others set on the beach, casting a warm glow along the sand. Since the space right in front of the bar was limited, thick, comfortable blankets had been spread out on the dry sand for patrons to relax and enjoy their cocktails. Amidst the sounds of lapping waves, Sarah, Euclid, and Harry sat at a low rattan table.

"I must say, these coconut rum cocktails are simply divine," Sarah exclaimed, taking a sip of her drink.

Euclid grinned. "I tried to get the owner to tell me the secret ingredient, but she wouldn't budge."

Harry tasted her drink and chimed in, "I think I detect a hint of banana rum and brown sugar in here."

Euclid shook his head. "No, I'm telling you, I think it's a splash of condensed milk."

A stray ginger cat that had been rubbing against Sarah's legs for the last ten minutes decided to take a leap of faith and jumped up onto her lap. As she scratched the puss behind its ears, he purred and settled in for a nap. Laughter filled the air as they watched the antics of the little cat.

"Sarah, don't even think about taking him home," Euclid said, giving his girlfriend a playful but stern warning. He explained to Harry that Sarah was a bit of a 'crazy cat lady' and that they already had four rescues at home.

"Don't worry," Sarah said, continuing to scratch the little marmalade cat on her lap. "I think he's Rosie's. I saw her feeding him fresh shrimp when we arrived."

Euclid breathed a sigh of relief. He knew quite well that if the little fellow were homeless, Sarah would dedicate the rest of the vacation to finding him a new home or a shelter.

"Have you met Clara?" Sarah asked, deciding to change the topic.

Harry shook her head. "No, I haven't had a chance to meet her yet. How is she?"

"We saw her in Reception when we were going for a walk. She arrived this afternoon and has been with her mother at the hospital, giving her some emotional support."

Euclid added, "Yvonne must be grateful that Clara's here. She's been attending to Lisa tirelessly. I saw Yvonne briefly yesterday outside our hut; she was on her way to her house. She was a shadow of her former self. Dark shadows under her eyes and gaunt face. I don't think she's slept or eaten since James was taken to hospital."

"I suppose it's a huge blow to her, and to Marieke's business. If the news of the incident spreads, they may lose any future clients at the retreat. Even though it's not their fault, people don't want to stay in a place where someone—"

"Let's hope James pulls through," Euclid interrupted, not wanting his girlfriend to end her sentence.

As their conversation proceeded, the tone shifted, weighed down by the seriousness of recent events. Harry listened intently but refrained from sharing her own suspicions and concerns. She didn't want to break Marieke's trust. Suddenly, Sarah hushed their voices, pointing toward Clara and Amaya as they approached the bar from the direction of the retreat. Excitement mingled with anticipation as the group prepared to welcome them.

"Hi, Amaya! Clara, please come join us," Sarah called out, gesturing to an empty blanket next to her.

Amaya, with her dark hair cascading in loose curls, and Clara, with her vibrant blonde locks, approached the group. Sarah leaned in and whispered to Harry and Euclid, "Don't you think they look similar? They could be sisters."

Euclid raised an eyebrow, puzzled. "How so?"

Sarah nodded. "True, their hair colors are different, but look at their faces and physique. There's something strangely similar about them."

"Not sure I see any similarity," Euclid said, shaking his head.

As Amaya and Clara sat down, Sarah greeted them warmly. "Hi, Clara! It's nice to meet you. This is my boyfriend Euclid, and this is Harry. We're all at the same retreat as your parents."

"Nice to meet you, Clara," Harry said, waving at James's daughter. "How was your journey?"

Clara smiled, but her face showed signs of worry. "Thank you. It was a long trip from Chicago, with a layover in Bangkok. I'm glad to finally be here. I've always wanted to visit Thailand, but never suspected it would be under such terrible circumstances."

"It must be very hard, but we're very happy to see you here. Would you like one of these delicious cocktails?"

"Not sure if I feel festive," Clara responded. "But I'd love a whiskey with soda."

"And one of these lovely concoctions for me, please," Amaya said, making herself comfortable beside Sarah and petting the cat.

Euclid wandered off to the bar to get their drinks.

"I've had a terrible time for the last few days, unable to sleep and running on adrenaline and stress," Clara explained. "I think being on the plane for so many hours without any news was the worst. I dreaded turning my cell phone back on when we landed in Bangkok."

"It's wonderful of you to come and support your mother during this difficult time. I can't even imagine what you're going through." Sarah put her hand on Clara's shoulder.

"I had to be here. I couldn't live with myself if I left my mom alone in this situation. I can only stay for one drink with you guys, however, because I'm quite exhausted from the journey and from staying at the hospital all day," Clara said, nodding earnestly as she took her drink from Euclid. "But it's so nice to be able to talk about it."

"And how is your father? What did the doctors say?" Harry asked, concern evident in her voice.

Clara took a deep breath. "I went straight to the hospital as soon as I arrived in Samui. The doctors diagnosed him with a severe head injury, and he's currently in an induced coma to stop the brain swelling. They say it could be weeks before he wakes up, or he may never..."

The group fell silent, absorbing the terrible weight of the news. Harry then asked about Lisa. "How is your mother coping with all of this? We've not seen much of her as she's been either at the hospital, or in her hut with Yvonne. Yvonne's been bringing her food and making phone calls for her."

Clara's eyes welled up with tears. "My mother has been inconsolable. She hasn't stopped crying since my dad was taken to the hospital. When she's not at the hospital, she spends all her time refreshing her phone screen, anxiously waiting for any news or updates. I'm so thankful to Yvonne and Marieke for all their help. Without them, we'd struggle with the hospital admin and the language barrier. My dad's doctor speaks English, but not all the nurses who look after him do. It helps a lot to know what everyone is saying."

The weight of the unknown hung in the air, casting a somber shadow over the conversation. The group shared a solemn moment, realizing the gravity of the situation and the uncertainty that lay ahead for James and his family.

Clara took a sip of her drink and, feeling that she was among friends, decided to share more details about her family's life.

"My mom has been heartbroken because they had argued on the day of the accident, and she wasn't speaking to my father just before it happened. As always, it was about Helen."

"Helen?" Harry asked.

"My mom used to love the water, but two years ago, she was diagnosed with osteoarthritis. It's too painful for her to jump on and off a boat, and even to walk around the deck. Despite that, my dad got a new boat, *Helen of Troy*. That's when everything changed," she explained. "He became obsessed with the boat, spending all his time on it and neglecting our family. My mom felt like she lost him to that boat, and she resented it. It became a symbol of their growing distance."

Harry nodded in understanding. "I can imagine how difficult that must have been for your mom," she said sympathetically. "Sometimes, people get caught up in their passions and unintentionally neglect the ones they love. It's unfortunate that they argued right before the accident."

Clara looked down, her voice filled with sadness. "I wish they had a chance to make things right," she says. "Now, my mom blames herself for not speaking to him that day. She feels guilty that they ended the day on a sour note."

Harry reached out to comfort Clara. "Accidents happen, and we can't predict them," she said gently. "It's important for your mom to understand that she couldn't have known what would happen. What matters now is that we support each other through this difficult time."

Clara gave a weak smile. "Thank you for saying that," she said. "It's just hard to accept sometimes. Some days, I feel like I'm in a movie. You know, like I'm watching myself do things, but I don't recognize the circumstances. Nothing makes sense."

"You're not alone in this, Clara. We're all here for you and your mom. We'll get through it together," Harry reassured her.

They sat in silence for a moment, lost in their thoughts. Harry felt a sense of relief that *Helen* was a boat not a mistress.

To lighten the mood, Sarah turned to Clara and Amaya. "Hey ladies, how about we go for a scooter ride across the jungle tomorrow morning? It'll be a fun adventure and a great way to clear our heads."

Amaya gave Sarah a quizzical look as if questioning the idea. "Surely, Sarah, you don't think that—" she began, before Clara interjected.

"Thank you, Sarah. I'd love to go on a scooter ride. It sounds like just what I need to take my mind off things."

Sarah turned to Harry, her eyes filled with anticipation. "What about you, Harry? Will you join us?"

Harry smiled and nodded. "Absolutely, count me in. I used to ride a dirtbike when I was a teenager. A scooter is not the same, but I love the sense of freedom, and I've been admiring the jungle hills behind us since I arrived on the island. I'd love to explore them."

After finishing his second coconut cocktail, Euclid put on a mock, sullen expression. "Oh, so I'll be all by myself then? No one to keep me company," he said, pretending to be upset.

Sarah chuckled. "Come on, Euclid, you know you'd secretly enjoy some alone time. You'll be able to finish your book of math puzzles in peace and quiet."

Euclid could not help but smile. "That's true. With everything that has been happening, I've not had a quiet moment to myself."

The group laughed, and the tension momentarily lifted as they enthusiastically accepted the idea of a scooter ride through the jungle. It would be a brief respite from the worries that surrounded them.

After the women had agreed to go on a scooter ride the following day, Euclid raised his hand to signal the bartender for another round of coconut rum cocktails. The atmosphere at the beach bar was cheerful and relaxed. Harry saw this as the perfect moment to address the matter of the black sarong she had found earlier.

"By the way, Amaya," Harry began, her voice carrying over the lively chatter. "I found a black sarong earlier. It looks just like the one you wore on the boat trip."

Amaya's brow furrowed. "My sarong? Where did you find it?" she asked, her confusion evident.

"It was in the mangrove near Captain Lamai's boat. I figured you left it on her boat, and it must have flown away."

Harry reached into her satchel and retrieved a plastic bag containing the sarong. She held it out for Amaya to see. "This one," she clarified, her gaze fixed on Amaya's reaction. "I took it to my hut and dried it, and then I thought I'd bring it along in case you came to the bar. I was going to drop it off at your hut if I didn't see you here."

Amaya's eyes widened as she examined the fabric. "Oh, it's identical, but it's not mine. It can't be."

Harry's confusion grew. "Not yours?" she echoed, surprised. "But it looks just like the one you were wearing on the boat trip."

Amaya nodded, her voice resolute. "I understand the confusion. It looks like mine, but isn't. I have mine in my hut in my suitcase; I saw it there when I was getting dressed to come here tonight. It's a popular design that can be found in any street market on the island. It's possible that someone else from the retreat owns a sarong like this one. Or, as you say, it flew away from one of the boats. It could be anyone's. But they're not very expensive, so I don't think the owner would be worried about it. Maybe leave it in the reception area, in case it belongs to someone from the retreat."

"Good idea," Harry agreed, but her curiosity was piqued. She wondered if it might be a deliberate attempt to frame Amaya, or someone else for that matter.

Chapter 16

THROUGH THE JUNGLE

The next morning, the four women gathered in the parking area outside the retreat's reception. The gentle sound of the sea served as a soothing backdrop to their conversation. Harry, Sarah, Clara, and Amaya were joined by Marieke, who approached them, along with one of her staff members. The atmosphere was filled with excitement.

"Good morning, everyone," Marieke said with a warm smile. "I hope you're all ready for an adventurous scooter ride through the jungle."

"This is Nop," Marieke added, introducing her staff member. "He will be your guide for the day."

Nop offered a friendly greeting, his voice reflecting the serene nature of the island. "Hello, ladies," he said, bowing slightly. "I will be leading you on an incredible scooter route so you can see the natural beauty of Koh Samui."

The women returned his greeting with enthusiasm, eager to embark on the adventure. Nop explained the route, commenting on some notable highlights they would see along the way.

"We will ride through the jungle trails, passing through natural coconut groves," Nop began, his voice filled with enthusiasm. "Our first stop will be at an elephant sanctuary, where you'll have the opportunity to interact with the elephants and learn about the sanctuary's conservation efforts."

Mention of the elephant sanctuary elicited excited murmurs from the group.

"From there, we'll continue our ride along a scenic coastal road," Nop continued, a hint of pride in his voice. "You'll see breathtaking views of some amazing beaches and the turquoise waters that make Koh Samui so famous."

Harry's eyes sparkled with anticipation. She couldn't wait to immerse herself in the natural wonders of the island and explore its hidden gems.

Nop concluded, "Throughout our journey, I will ensure your safety and guide you to some of the most picturesque spots on the island. So, enjoy the ride, take in the beauty of Koh Samui, and have a wonderful adventure. We have already prepared the scooters for you."

"These bikes are for Amaya, Sarah, and Clara," Marieke said, assigning the scooters. "And this one is for you, Harry. You told me that you have ridden before, so this one has a bit of a bigger engine." Each woman was given a key and a helmet.

As the group prepared to set off on their scooters, the morning sun cast a fresh golden glow over the scene. With hearts full of excitement and curiosity, they mounted their metal steeds, ready to explore the island.

As the buzzing scooters weaved through the bustling streets of Koh Samui town, Harry couldn't help but take in the action unfolding around her. The roads were filled with a symphony of sounds—the revving of scooters, the honking of tuk-tuks, and the chatter of street vendors. The tantalizing aroma of street food wafted through the air, tempting the passersby with tasty snacks.

Amongst the busy traffic, Harry noticed children being transported to school on colorful scooters, their laughter and excited chatter filling the air. Tuk-tuk drivers called out to tourists, offering rides and enticing them with promises of an authentic Thai experience. The air was thick with humidity. Yellow trumpet flowers and bushes of pink bougainvillea lined the roadside, adding a splash of color to the passing parade.

As the group left the chaotic streets of the town behind them and began ascending the green slopes of the mountains, their environment magically transformed into a serene and picturesque landscape. Dense foliage surrounded them, providing a quiet respite from the bustling towns and villages. Overtaking a Jeep filled with enthusiastic tourists, Harry caught sight of some young backpackers sitting on the roof of the vehicle. Oblivious to the danger, they were shouting hellos and waving cheerfully at the passing scooters.

However, the momentary distraction of some boys goofing around couldn't fully lift the weight from Harry's mind. She found herself slipping back into the web of suspicions and unanswered questions surrounding James's accident. Each suspect flitted through her thoughts like a passing shadow.

At times, Harry's mind raced as fast as her scooter's engine as she tried to connect each observation she had made, but the truth eluded her. She couldn't shake the feeling that the answer lay hidden within the secrets that her companions had held back from her thus far.

Lost in her thoughts, the scooter ride became a mere backdrop to her morning as she grappled with the mystery that lay before her. The road ahead seemed to stretch endlessly, with blind rises and twists and turns through the jungle, mirroring the path she had embarked upon in the hope of unravelling the truth behind the events that had shaken their peaceful retreat in Thailand.

As the scooters ventured deeper into the pristine jungle of Koh Samui, Harry spotted towering trees and stunning heliconia flowers. The air was thick with the sweet scent of orchids and fruit trees.

Lost in the beauty of her surroundings, Harry allowed her thoughts to settle on the suspects she needed to evaluate. The first category she focused on was the local staff members of the retreat. Their connection to James and Lisa seemed more rooted in the undertaking of their professional roles, making it unlikely that they would harbor a personal grudge deep enough to compel them to hurt James. The crime demanded intimate knowledge of and proximity to the victim, factors that were less likely to be exploited by the local staff.

Harry then shifted her attention to Mary, who had performed life-saving CPR on James moments after the incident. It struck Harry as highly improbable that someone who wished James harm would be willing to intervene as she did and potentially save his life. If Mary had harbored ill intentions toward James, her actions seemed contradictory to her supposed motives. Harry reasoned that Mary could have stayed silent and allowed him to perish in front of everyone. Her behavior didn't align with the profile of a cold-blooded attacker.

Pleased with her logical deductions, Harry felt a sense of relief as she crossed Mary off her list of suspects. It was a small victory in her quest for truth. With Mary now eliminated, Harry found herself grappling with the next set of potential culprits.

Lisa, James's wife, seemed to be genuinely distraught after the accident, and her daughter's accounts indicated a complex but ultimately loving relationship between the couple. Despite her instinct telling her that Lisa was unlikely to be involved, Harry decided to keep her on the suspect list, just to be thorough.

Turning her attention to the two men, Harry considered their possible motives. Anthony stood out as the more likely suspect. He had expressed a clear disdain for James from the beginning of their stay at the retreat, attributing his serious financial losses to advisors like him. Although James wasn't directly responsible for Anthony's misfortune, bitterness could have driven Anthony to contemplate taking drastic measures in the form of revenge.

Harry couldn't ignore her growing suspicions about Anthony's intense interest in the case; his insistence that it was Lisa and his persistent surveillance of her and Marieke. It raised questions about his true intentions and his potential involvement in the events surrounding James's accident. Even though she considered Anthony a friend, she needed to keep him on her list of potential killers.

And then there was Euclid. Of all the people at the retreat, Harry found him to be the most transparent and therefore innocent. His background was easily verifiable, as everyone knew where he worked and where his family came from. Harry was certain that a quick Google search would yield his face on a faculty page of the college he mentioned, with his father's reputation preceding him. Euclid didn't fit the profile of a suspect in her mind. What could his motive be for wanting to harm James? Nothing in his history indicated any connection to James or any reason to harm him. With a sense of conviction, Harry crossed Euclid off her list of suspects.

However, a nagging feeling crept into her mind. Despite her initial trust in Euclid, Harry made a mental note to break the retreat's rules and go online that night to verify the authenticity of everyone's credentials. She realized that if they truly were who they claimed to be, there would be some trace of their presence on some social media platform. As a travel blogger, she understood the digital footprint people left behind and that it was rare for someone to have no online presence whatsoever. Tonight would be the night to investigate further and ensure that each person at the retreat was who they portrayed themselves to be.

With a plan in mind and the suspects narrowed down, Harry considered the remaining women at the retreat: Sarah and Amaya. Like Euclid's, Sarah's identity seemed to be easily verifiable via her school's website, but her adoption presented a potential link to James that Harry couldn't ignore. Could there be a hidden family secret related to Sarah's adoption? Was there a connection between James and her adoptive parents? Harry made a mental note to dig deeper into Sarah's background, hoping to uncover any potential connections or grievances.

Then there was Amaya, a woman with an unverifiable identity and a mysterious past. Her occupation as a globetrotting house sitter raised Harry's suspicions. It seemed like the perfect cover for someone involved in shady activities. And Amaya's dark past, with a father who died in a tragic accident, added another layer of intrigue. Perhaps there was more to it. What if he hadn't died, but, instead, had abandoned them? The question of her father's identity lingered, and Harry couldn't help but wonder if James could be connected to Amaya's painful past in some way.

Harry paused for a moment, contemplating the idea. Could a father forget his own daughter's face after abandoning her and causing so much pain? "Maybe," Harry answered to herself aloud. It was a grim thought, but Harry reasoned that if James was truly a cold-hearted man who had left his young family in such dire circumstances, he might not remember a four-year-old girl after all those years. Children's faces change as they grow older. Harry felt a sense of sadness as she considered the possibility, but she couldn't dwell on it for long.

"What were you saying?"

Her train of thought was interrupted by Amaya overtaking on her scooter, calling out to Harry. Startled, Harry quickly composed herself and replied, "Just talking to myself!" She hoped that Amaya hadn't overheard her speculative thoughts, allowing her suspicions to remain concealed for now.

Chapter 17

ELEPHANT SANCTUARY

As the group entered the elephant sanctuary, Harry set aside her speculations, determined to enjoy the experience and take a break from her investigative thoughts. The group was greeted by one of the sanctuary's caretakers, Anong, who was passionate about the majestic creatures that resided there.

"As you may have heard from tour guides during your stay in Thailand, elephants hold significant cultural and historical importance to our country," Anong began. "They were once revered as sacred animals and played a vital role in the country's traditions and festivals." She explained that the sanctuary's mission was to provide a safe and ethical environment for these gentle giants.

"How long do elephants typically live?" Amaya asked as soon as Anong finished her presentation on the sanctuary.

"In the wild, elephants can live up to 60 or 70 years. However, here in the sanctuary, where they receive exceptional care, they often live even longer."

"Are elephants really as intelligent as they say?" Sarah asked.

Anong nodded in affirmation. "Absolutely! Elephants are known for their remarkable intelligence. They have an incredible memory and are capable of complex social interactions. They even mourn the loss of their loved ones, showing deep emotions."

As they continued their walk through the sanctuary, the women witnessed the staff engaging with the elephants, feeding them, and washing them with gentle care. The sight of the massive creatures enjoying the cool water brought smiles to their faces.

Clara, unable to contain her enthusiasm, asked, "Can we help feed them?"

Anong's eyes lit up, happy to oblige. "Of course! It's an interactive experience. Follow me, and you can give them some of their favorite treats."

The group gathered around as the caretaker distributed baskets filled with fruits and vegetables. They approached the elephants cautiously, extending their hands to offer the delicious snacks. The elephants reached out with their trunks, their touch both gentle and powerful, as they accepted the treats.

Harry watched on in awe. Her encounter with these magnificent creatures served as a moment of welcome distraction from her ongoing investigation. The connection between the humans and the elephants felt special and resonated with her appreciation for the beauty and grandeur of nature.

As the women fed the elephants, Sarah observed Harry's distracted demeanor. She moved closer to her and asked, "Hey, you seem rather preoccupied today. Is everything alright?"

"Oh, just a bit worried about Captain Lamai. There's been no news. Marieke called her grandmother, but she hasn't returned home." Harry replied, carefully feeding a giant slice of watermelon to an elephant.

"If I disappeared for just one night, my parents would lose their minds. Wouldn't yours?" Sarah commented, unaware of the blunder.

"You still live with your parents? Even when you're back in the US?" Harry asked to divert the conversation away.

Sarah chuckled and explained, "Yes, I do. The real estate prices in Chicago are sky-high, and I'm still figuring out where I want to settle down. Besides, I travel and work abroad a lot, so it just makes sense for now. I don't spend a lot of time there, mostly to store my clothes and books in my old bedroom. My mom kept it as it was when I left for college. It can be very embarrassing to have friends over, not to mention a boyfriend."

"Your parents must miss you a lot," Harry observed.

Sarah rolled her eyes playfully and responded, "Oh, they miss me way too much. Being an adopted child means they've always been a bit overprotective. They worry about me all the time, but they can also be quite controlling. I always had to be the best at everything and compete in everything. As a child I barely had any time to myself—it was always violin classes, French lessons, or gymnastics training. It came easily to me so I did it to make them happy. To see the smile on their faces whenever I won a trophy or an award was priceless. Our living room is a shrine to my youthful accomplishments—it's bit over-the-top, but I love them too much to tell them to take it down."

Harry smiled sympathetically as the women continued feeding the elephants.

"That's sweet to have such caring parents. What do they do?" Clara asked.

"They run a small veterinarian clinic. It's not easy competing with the big franchises, but they have faithful clients who trust no one else with their beloved pets," Sarah proudly replied. "I used to work there when I was in high school. At first, I just cleaned the cages and fed the pets that were in our care, but then I was taught how to groom dogs. I quite enjoyed it. Except for a few bitey Yorkies, most of my four-legged beauties were very happy with their haircuts."

Harry, reminiscing about her own lifestyle, admitted, "You know, one thing about being a digital nomad is that I miss having a furry companion. I'd love to have a cat or a dog, but with all the constant traveling, it wouldn't be fair on them. Dogs and cats need a routine."

Sarah signaled her agreement. "Absolutely. Pets thrive on routine and stability. It's a big commitment, and it wouldn't be fair to leave them behind or disrupt their lives."

"Pet sitting is how I get to travel around the world," Amaya interjected. "People like their pets to stay home in their own beds and on their old sofas."

Their conversation paused as Anong brought a couple of baby elephants to taste the fruit. Harry's heart was warmed by the gentle giants standing before her. The bond between the animals and humans was uplifting.

"Do you enjoy doing pet and house-sitting? It sounds like a unique way to live like a local," Sarah asked Amaya.

"Oh, absolutely! It's such a fun way to immerse yourself in different cultures. When it comes to pets, I love all the animals, but I prefer looking after dogs. Dogs let you know what they want and stay close all the time." Amaya paused for a moment, remembering past experiences. "Cats, on the other hand, can be a bit more challenging. They can be finicky, and some are very talented escape artists. It can get quite stressful for a pet-sitter to look after a cat that likes to run around at night. I don't usually let them out because I worry that they won't come back home. Last time, I ended up with three bored tomcats pacing the apartment and meowing all day to be let out. Then, at night, they were jumping up and down on me as if I were a human trampoline, asking me for snacks even though their bowls were filled with dry food. I had to get up at 5 a.m. every morning to open their tuna tins, or the big one, Milo, would purr and meow right in my face until I woke up."

Amaya's companion chuckled at her cat-sitting story.

"Did you have any pets when you were a child?" Clara asked.

Amaya's face darkened momentarily as her memories resurfaced. She shook her head and cut this branch of the conversation short, saying, "No, unfortunately not. My mom wasn't in the right state of mind to look after me or my little brother, let alone a pet. But that's why I enjoy pet-sitting now. It allows me to give love and care to animals while experiencing different parts of the world."

Amaya turned to Harry. "If you miss having a pet, you should try signing up on a pet and house-sitting website. You can work on your travel blog *and* spend time with dogs and cats. It's a cheap way to travel the world and have furry companionship at the same time."

Harry considered Amaya's suggestion and said, "You know, that could be a really fun way to travel! And it would certainly help with my budget."

"Does being a travel blogger provide you with a good income?" Clara asked rather directly.

Harry smiled mysteriously and admitted, "Making money from travel writing requires a lot of time and ingenuity. Fortunately, when I turned 21, I inherited a trust fund from my parents. It's just enough to cover my flights and travel expenses each month, but I still need to supplement it with my writing."

Clara, hearing the mention of a trust fund, let out a whistle and asked, "So, you have wealthy parents?"

Amaya, aware of Harry's painful past, jumped in quickly to clarify the matter. "Harry's parents died when she was a child..."

"I'm so sorry," Clara sounded genuinely mortified by her *faux pas.*

Harry reassured Clara, "No need to apologize. You couldn't have known. My family's circumstances were a bit more complicated, but I'm grateful for the support I have now. When my parents passed away, I received a substantial life insurance payout, which was placed in a trust fund by my grandparents."

Harry's voice filled with genuine interest as she steered the conversation back to less sensitive issues. "Did *you* have any pets growing up?"

Clara's face lit up with a nostalgic smile. "Oh, how I wished we had a furry friend! But unfortunately, my parents weren't too keen on the idea of having a dog inside the house. My dad used to work long hours, and my mom was always busy with parent associations and women's clubs. She was very house-proud and hosted loads of events and parties. I supposed a muddy pooch was not part of her vision of a perfect home."

"Your parents seem to be very connected. Were they high school sweethearts?" Sarah asked, curious about James and Lisa's love story.

Clara shook her head, her eyes sparkling with fond memories.

"Can you believe it?" Clara exclaimed with a hint of amusement in her voice. "They were both in their late twenties when their paths crossed in a hostel in Florence. It was like a meeting of kindred spirits. They instantly clicked and decided to continue their European journey together."

Amaya grinned mischievously. "That's straight out of a romantic comedy! Two wanderlust souls finding love in the midst of their globetrotting."

Clara nodded enthusiastically. "Exactly! Their photos from their backpacking years always bring laughter to our family gatherings. My dad had these long blond dreadlocks and a Robinson Crusoe beard. It's quite the contrast to the clean-shaven, smartly dressed man we know him as now."

Sarah burst into laughter. "James with a beard and dreadlocks? That's quite the image! He always appears so polished and professional."

Clara laughed, her eyes gleaming with fondness. "I know, right? And my mom used to wear beads in her hair, and long hippy skirts. They were quite the hardcore hippies, those two, even though it was the late 1990s."

The young women giggled at the contrast and the transformation Clara's parents had undergone over the years. Sarah sighed wistfully. "It sounds like a dream, Clara. The freedom, the adventure, and the romance. I envy their experiences."

Clara agreed wholeheartedly. "Oh, it was truly something special. By the time they settled back home, they had traveled all over Europe and South America. They had seen

Machu Picchu, Chichén Itzá, and the beaches of Buenos Aires. Very romantic, too. But my favorite photo of them is from Amsterdam. My dad proposed to my mom on this cute little bridge over a canal. She was sitting on an old-fashioned rusty bicycle that had a basket filled with tulips, and my dad was on one knee in front of her. They must have been in their late twenties. It's a moment frozen in time, so sweet."

Clara's eyes sparkled with nostalgia.

"It sounds like a scene from a fairytale," Harry said, captivated by the heartfelt story. But something in Clara's account of her parents' past was bothering her. Something about their travels wasn't adding up. She had a vague recollection of either James or Lisa telling her that they had never been outside of the US. *Why would they lie about it?*

As the conversation wound down, Nop appeared, asking if they were ready to continue to the next stop on their trip. Expressing their gratitude for the unforgettable experience, they all thanked Anong and promised to spread the word about the sanctuary to help with its fundraising for the old and sick elephants. As they approached the scooters, Clara absentmindedly approached Harry's as if it were hers, unaware of the mix-up.

Wanting to avoid any awkwardness, Harry decided not to mention the mistake and focused on Nop's instructions instead. He explained that they would now head to a stunning waterfall, warning them of the steep downhill slopes they would traverse along the way. He advised them to ride slowly and use their bikes' back and front brakes at the same time.

With this thoughtful advice in mind, the group prepared to resume their journey. Harry, who was used to riding off-road, was ready to navigate the challenging terrain ahead. As they set off, they proceeded with caution, their minds filled with a sense of adventure.

Chapter 18

The Fall

As they rode on their scooters, Clara's mind was preoccupied with worry, her thoughts consumed by her father's condition. The earlier conversation about her parents and their romantic life together had stirred up a deep sense of sad nostalgia. She feared the worst, imagining a future without her father, and the burden it would place on her mother. The weight of responsibility felt heavy on her shoulders as she contemplated how she would support and comfort her mother through such a difficult time.

Lost in thought, Clara was abruptly jolted out of her reverie as she realized that her scooter was rapidly picking up speed as she descended the hill. Panic surged through her veins, and her anxiety intensified. She held on to the handlebars tightly, her heart racing with a mix of fear and adrenaline. The wind rushed past her, adding to the sensation of being out of control.

As Clara hurtled down the hill, she frantically attempted to activate the back brake, desperately hoping to slow down, but to her horror, nothing happened. The scooter continued to gather speed, careening down the hill with an alarming velocity.

Fear gripped Clara's entire being as she tried to apply the back brake repeatedly, her actions becoming more frantic with each failed attempt. She watched helplessly as her scooter overtook the others, her voice drowned out by the rushing wind. The guide's shouts urging her to use the brakes only intensified her desperation.

In panic, Clara decided to take a gamble and pulled on the front brake, hoping against hope that it would bring the scooter to a stop. But instead of slowing down, a terrifying realization washed over her as the front wheel locked up, causing the scooter to pitch forward violently.

In an instant, the world around Clara became a whirlwind of chaos. She was thrown into the air, the force of inertia launching her from the vehicle. Time seemed to stretch and slow down as she tumbled through the air.

Chapter 19

DARK THOUGHTS

Her thoughts swirled with sinister satisfaction, a wicked grin playing at the corners of her lips. As the clock ticked closer to two in the afternoon, a sense of anticipation filled her mind. There was no news from the women on their scooters or the guide, but she was hopeful that her plan was working, just as she had meticulously orchestrated. A flicker of triumph danced in her eyes.

Harry, the relentless investigator, would soon be out of the picture. No more snooping, no more prying questions that threatened to unravel the carefully woven web of deceit. She had become an obstacle, a thorn in their side, and it had been time to remove her from the equation. The woman's heart was pounding with a mix of regret and relief at the prospect of finally silencing her once and for all.

A brief feeling of remorse lingered momentarily, leaving a bitter taste in the woman's mouth. Yes, she admitted to herself, it had been a mistake involving Harry in the first place. A momentary lapse in judgment that had almost cost her everything. But now she had rectified that error, sealing Harry's fate with a carefully laid trap.

No one will miss that little millennial snowflake, the woman thought, trying to justify her actions to herself. *She had no children, and her parents have long been dead. It had to be done.*

A twisted sense of triumph washed over her as she imagined Harry confined to a bed, her holiday dreams shattered. She would be forced to face the consequences of crossing their path, paying the price for her relentless pursuit of the truth. In her twisted mind, it was a fitting punishment.

As the minutes ticked by, the woman's anxiety grew. The plan had been set in motion, and now all she could do was wait for the news of Harry's unfortunate accident. *It was regrettable*, she thought. *Harry seemed like a smart and friendly girl. In another time and place, they could have been friends, but she had to stop her before she found the attacker.*

Chapter 20

In the Jungle

Clara opened her eyes slowly and found her vision to be blurred and hazy. The vivid blue sky stretched out above her, adorned with fluffy white clouds. As her gaze wandered, the foliage of the surrounding jungle came into focus. Coconut palm leaves swayed playfully in the warm breeze.

Disorientation washed over Clara's mind as she tried to make sense of her surroundings. *Where am I? Is this a dream?* She questioned herself; the surreal beauty of the scene around her left her feeling stunned. Instead of being relaxed, a deep sense of premotion washed over her. Something sinister was lurking behind the beautiful tableaux. With a mix of trepidation, she closed her eyes once more, hoping that when she opened them again, she would find herself in her bed. The alarm on her bedside table would be ringing to let her know it was time to go to work.

But as Clara opened her eyes again, reality sank in. She wasn't dreaming. The colors, the sounds, the feeling of the tropical warm air against her skin—they were all too vivid, too tangible to be anything but real.

A flicker of fear danced across Clara's chest, uncertainty casting a shadow over her thoughts. *Where am I? How did I get here?* The questions swirled in her mind, searching for answers that eluded her grasp. She tried to recall the events leading up to this moment, but her memory was foggy, with fragments of images and sensations slipping through her fingers.

Clara took a deep breath to steady herself; she hoped to find a sense of grounding amidst the uncertainty of her situation. Feeling incredibly tired, she closed her eyes again. Soon, a medley of unfamiliar voices appeared out of nowhere.

"Clara! Clara! Wake up!" a female voice was demanding.

Someone was holding her hand and sobbing. A male voice was muttering in an unfamiliar language. *Where are these voices coming from?* Clara wondered.

She started to feel cold. Colder than she had ever felt in her life. The cold was inside her body, chilling her from the inside.

"She's shivering," another female voice shouted. "There's nothing to cover her with."

"She needs help soon."

Clara's head felt heavy, and she struggled to focus on the faces above her. The voices were muffled, and she couldn't make sense of what they were saying.

"Clara! Stay with us, okay?" Harry's voice broke through the haze, but Clara couldn't find words to respond.

Amaya's urgent voice rose above the others, her eyes filled with tears. "Nop, we need an ambulance! Hurry!"

Nop looked flustered, but quickly pulled out his phone to call for help. Sarah's hands were trembling as she stroked Clara's head gently. "Clara, you're going to be okay. Just stay with us," she pleaded, trying to hide the fear in her voice.

Clara's vision started to clear a little, and she could see the worry etched on the faces around her. "What... happened?" she managed to whisper, her voice shaky.

"You had an accident. Your scooter... it flipped over," Harry explained.

Amaya added, "You lost control. We're so sorry, Clara."

Clara's eyes widened as she processed the information. Scraps of the moment just before her fall started to come back to her. "Back brake... I tried to slow down, but it didn't work," she murmured. "I pulled it and pulled it so many times."

Nop, visibly upset, called Harry over.

"Is help on the way?" she asked.

"I can't catch a cellphone signal here. I've tried all around here," he declared with deep worry in his voice. "But I've been thinking that even if we manage to make the call, it will be hard to explain to the paramedics where to find us. It could take hours. I'm going to ride down as fast as I can and go directly to the hospital. I'll be back with the paramedics."

Harry understood that it was the best plan. She looked back at the women kneeling by Clara and gestured for Nop to hurry. She returned to the group and explained Nop's plan.

Sarah's tears started to fall, and she looked away, unable to bear seeing Clara in pain. "I'm so sorry, Clara. This is all my fault. I shouldn't have suggested the scooter ride," she said, her voice filled with guilt and regret.

Clara tried to reach out to comfort Sarah, but a sharp, throbbing pain stopped her. "I can't move my arm."

At that moment, Harry took charge, trying to keep everyone calm. "Clara, your arm is probably broken; that's why you can't move it. You fell on your side and hit the ground very hard. But we're here with you," she said, and braced herself for an interminably long wait. As soon as the adrenaline wore off, Clara was going to be in a lot of pain.

In the dense jungle, the air was heavy with humidity and the sounds of unseen creatures. Clara remained lying on the ground, her face contorted with pain. Harry knelt beside her, keeping Clara's mind occupied with trivial stories from her travels. She was not an expert on first aid, but she had a strong intuition that it was essential to keep Clara awake in case she had sustained a serious head injury.

While Harry kept the superficial chit-chat going, her mind raced. It was clear that it should have been her, not Clara, who had the accident. *But why would Marieke do that?* The more Harry thought about it, the angrier she got. *It made no sense for Marieke to want her dead.*

As time stretched, Amaya paced nervously, occasionally glancing at the thick foliage surrounding them. She muttered to herself, "Where is Nop? He should have been back by now."

Clara's breathing was shallow, and her face had gone pale. Harry, her voice quivering with concern, said, "Clara, try to stay awake. Nop will be back soon with help."

Clara nodded weakly, her eyes darting around the unfamiliar jungle. She wasn't used to this kind of environment, and the pain in her arm was overwhelming. Looking at the young woman, who was in anguish, Harry hatched a plan to catch the person who sabotaged the scooter.

Chapter 21

CONFESSION

Outside Lisa's hut, the air was heavy with uncertainty. She took a deep breath, steeling herself for what lay ahead. With her heart pounding, Lisa set off for Mary's accommodation. She gathered what courage she had left and finally knocked on the hut's door. Moments later, Mary answered and ushered her inside. Lisa sat down on the edge of the bed, gazing out at the landscape through the window. Her eyes were red, a testament to the countless tears shed in the past few days.

Observing Lisa's fragile state, Mary spoke softly. "Lisa?"

Lisa turned her head, mustering a weak smile for her friend. "Mary, it's nice to see you. Please, sit down with me."

Taking a chair from the corner of the hut, Mary couldn't help but feel the severity of the situation. She knew that no words could truly ease Lisa's pain, but she needed to try.

"How are you holding up?" Mary asked, her voice filled with sympathy.

"It's been... it's been so hard, Mary. James hasn't woken up, and I don't know what to do. I wanted to talk to someone. And more than anything else, I wanted to thank you for saving James's..." Lisa's voice started to quiver, and she could not finish her sentence. "If it wasn't for you..."

Mary sat by Lisa on the bed and put an arm around her. "Don't think about it. I wish I had been there sooner. I can't even imagine what you're going through, Lisa. But you have a lot of support here. Everyone cares about you and James."

Lisa, her eyes welling with tears, whispered, "I appreciate that, Mary. It just feels like my whole world has turned upside down. We were supposed to have this amazing vacation together and..."

Mary patted Lisa gently on her shoulder to comfort her. "I know, Lisa. Life can be so unpredictable."

In the quiet of the room, both women grappled with dark thoughts. Mary offered her support, saying, "If there's anything I can do, please don't hesitate to ask. Even if you just need someone to talk to."

Lisa's gratitude was palpable as she replied, "Thank you, Mary. I might take you up on that."

The two women spoke softly about their worries and hopes for James. But their comforting words and uncertain sighs were interrupted when they heard a violent knock on the door. Before Mary could say anything, the door opened, and Anthony abruptly entered the room. His face was drained of color.

"Anthony, what's wrong?" Lisa asked, concern lacing her voice.

"Sorry to come like this, but I've just received an urgent message," Anthony explained.

"What's wrong? Have you got news of James?" Lisa stood up, concerned about what had brought Anthony here.

Anthony struggled to find his words. "No, it's not about James. There's been an accident during the jungle scooter ride. One of the girls is badly injured. We need to get to the hospital right away. I've already spoken to Euclid. He's just left with Marieke and Yvonne in case an interpreter is needed."

Panic gripped Lisa as she realized her daughter had gone on the scooter ride.

"Oh, no! Clara!" she cried.

Without hesitation, they rushed out of the hut and towards the main entrance to the retreat, where a line of tuk-tuks was awaiting passing tourists. Anthony felt an uneasy knot in his stomach as they climbed aboard one and headed off to the hospital. The colorful streets of Koh Samui passed by in a blur, filled with a chaotic mix of scooters, cars, and other tuk-tuks. The warm breeze tousled the passengers' hair as they weaved swiftly through traffic. From his seat in the open-sided vehicle, Anthony could see bustling marketplaces where locals and tourists haggled over souvenirs and fresh produce. The tuk-tuk's motor roared, drowning out the cacophony of voices and music from the bars lining the road.

Anthony couldn't help but feel apprehensive, his mind racing with questions. *Why was Harry so cryptic about the accident in her message? Why did she tell him to summon everyone to the hospital? Why wasn't he allowed to mention who had been injured?* The whole situation felt off-kilter, and Anthony's instincts were telling him that something wasn't right, but he decided to trust the young woman. Soon enough, it would all become clear.

Koh Samui Hospital loomed ahead of them as the tuk-tuk slowed to a stop at the entrance to the emergency department. From the outside, the hospital appeared to be a modern, clean facility. The exterior was painted in a soothing shade of pale green, and the hospital's sign was adorned with both Thai and English lettering.

Inside the reception area, they spotted Marieke, Yvonne, and Euclid. The space was well-lit and airy, with a polished linoleum floor and rows of chairs occupied by waiting patients. A large aquarium with colorful fish provided a distraction for those who were waiting for medical attention. Marieke spoke to the receptionist in rapid Thai, her expression filled with worry. After a brief exchange, the nurse addressed the group. "The patient is stable and awaiting the results of her CT scan and X-ray," she informed them. "She'll be delighted to see some familiar faces. Please, follow me."

"Is it Sarah?" Euclid asked Yvonne as they followed the nurse.

"I'm not sure," Yvonne answered. "The nurse just said, 'young lady'."

Anthony stepped into the room and was immediately hit by the sterile, slightly chilling atmosphere that pervaded the ward. The fluorescent lights overhead gave the surroundings an unnatural, washed-out hue. His eyes darted to the figure lying on her side, facing away from the door, motionless on the bed. The patient's face was partially shrouded beneath a pristine white sheet.

Marieke rushed forward past Anthony, her voice trembling with worry. "Harry! Harry! Are you okay?" Her concern was palpable.

"I'm fine, Marieke," Harry responded from the corridor behind the group.

"It's me," Clara said, gingerly lifting the sheet with her good arm. "Mom?"

Lisa darted to her daughter's side, fighting back tears.

"Clara, darling, are you alright?" Lisa's voice trembled with anxiety as she bombarded her daughter with questions.

Clara, despite her evident discomfort, managed a small, reassuring smile. "I'll be okay, Mom," she said in a soothing tone. "I got some painkillers in the ambulance. I'm waiting for the results of the CT scan; I hit my head really hard. And then some X-rays to see how badly my arm is broken. But I'm feeling so much better right now. The girls were wonderful, keeping me company, and Nop is my hero."

"But where is Sarah?" Euclid asked, confused.

"I'm here." Sarah was right behind Harry and Amaya as they entered the room.

Euclid rushed to embrace his girlfriend.

In the tense hospital room, Harry stepped forward, her voice steady and confident. She explained how Clara's terrible fall had been due to a complete malfunction of the back brakes on her scooter. The room filled with gasps and sobs as the news sunk in. Mary's eyes widened in shock, and Lisa couldn't hold back her tears.

"What? Malfunctioning brakes?" Mary exclaimed. "Oh, dear! On these steep hills? Where did you get these scooters from? You must sue the rental company."

"They came from our retreat," Marieke stammered. "I'll investigate the scooter issue as soon as we get back. "

Harry, however, was unyielding. "Before you do that, Marieke, let's address another pressing matter. Why did you assume it was me lying there?" She fixed Marieke with a pointed stare, demanding an explanation.

Marieke, defensive in her tone, tried to explain her assumption. "Well, under the sheets, the body shape, it looked like..." Her voice trailed off as she struggled to find words.

"Seriously, Marieke?" Harry rolled her eyes, not buying the explanation. "Wasn't it you who prepared and designated the scooters to each of us before we departed?"

Sarah nodded in agreement. "That's true. You did hand out the scooters."

Harry stepped forward, her voice firm and unwavering. "I have a strong feeling you wanted to silence me, Marieke. You're trying to stop me from investigating James's attempted murder." She let her words hang in the air, a bold accusation that left everyone in the room in a tense silence.

Lisa, her voice tinged with concern and confusion, spoke up from her place by her daughter's side. She couldn't comprehend why they were talking about an attempted murder. "I don't understand," she stammered. "James was hit by a coconut. It was an accident."

"Yes, Harry, could you please explain? I thought it was just a bizarre accident," Mary chimed in, confused.

"It wasn't an accident. Someone tried to kill James and make it look like one."

Before anyone could react, Euclid's voice thundered, "Yvonne!" He leaped forward, arms outstretched, and managed to catch the fainting woman just before she crumpled to the unforgiving hospital floor.

A surge of panic rippled through the room, and Sarah bolted out of the door, her voice echoing down the corridor as she called for a nurse to help.

Mary knelt by Yvonne's side and began checking her vital signs. "Stay with me, Yvonne," she urged, trying to keep her composure amidst the growing tension.

A nurse came rushing into the room and swiftly assessed the situation. In a calm and reassuring tone, she asked Yvonne, who was gradually regaining consciousness, if she was okay and if she knew where she was.

Meanwhile, Mary had already placed a soft pillow beneath Yvonne's head, ensuring her comfort as she lay on the floor.

Another nurse came in and began checking Yvonne's vital signs and blood pressure.

Lisa, still holding her daughter's good hand and with a perplexed expression on her face, looked at Harry and hesitated before finally voicing her confusion. "Harry, please, can you explain what's going on?"

Harry began to respond, but Marieke abruptly interrupted her. Her voice, filled with both determination and simmering anger, cut through the room's tension like a knife. "You want to know? Fine, I'll tell you. Yes, I did try to kill that old scoundrel, James." Marieke's words hung heavily in the air, charged with pent-up resentment.

Lisa's eyes widened, and she gasped in disbelief. "What? James was hit by a coconut! It was an accident," she protested, shaking her head.

Marieke's face contorted with rage as she vehemently responded, "Accident? No, it wasn't! I recognized him on the second day of this cursed retreat. His investment company stole all my parents' money. They lost their home and became destitute during their retirement... and it was all because of him!"

The room fell into an uneasy silence as the weight of Marieke's revelation sank in. The confession had taken everyone by surprise, leaving them grappling with the sudden turn of events.

Marieke's voice trembled as she continued to explain her actions. "I couldn't stand the sight of him anymore," she confessed, her anger and frustration palpable. "Listening to his pompous tales of how rich and happy he was made me sick to my stomach."

She took a deep breath and continued, her voice steadier now. "During the mindfulness session, when everyone was facing the sea with their eyes closed, I saw my chance. I spotted James walking across the coconut plantation. It was the perfect opportunity."

Marieke's eyes revealed a mix of guilt and relief as she recounted her actions. "I grabbed a heavy metal hammer from the maintenance shed and snuck behind him. I hit him on the back of the head as hard as I could. He fell instantly," she admitted. "Then, I threw it away into the bushes. I grabbed a big coconut, wiped some blood onto it and placed it near his head to make it look like an accident."

Marieke's shocking confession was abruptly drowned out by a horrific shriek piercing the air. It had come from Lisa, who had completely lost control. All the emotions she had been bottling up over the past few days were now pouring out in a torrent of rage and despair.

Lisa's voice quivered with intense emotion as she screamed at Marieke, her words laced with anger and anguish. "You stupid, selfish woman! You've destroyed my life!" she accused, her eyes burning with fury. "You had no idea what kind of a man James was! How dare you judge us like this!"

Her voice cracked as she continued to vent her pent-up frustrations, her words echoing through the hospital room like a storm of emotions unleashed.

Amid the chaos, one of the nurses raised her voice above the commotion, demanding that everyone calm down immediately. Her commanding presence was undeniable. She added, in a somewhat quieter voice, that they all needed to leave the room for the sake of the patient.

Yvonne, still feeling a bit shaky, was then assisted into an armchair to ensure her well-being. In the background, a security guard stood watchfully.

As the group began to exit the room, Harry, with a sense of solemnity, approached Marieke and leaned in close to whisper in her ear, her words laced with a sense of finality.

"Is this how you want it to go down?" she asked.

Marieke, staring blankly at the floor, spoke in a hushed tone. "I'm sorry, Harry. I didn't want to kill you. I panicked."

As they walked into the reception area, Nop and two officers were awaiting them.

"Marieke, the police are here to take you to the station. They have some questions," he said as one of the officers put on handcuffs. Marieke didn't resist.

Anthony, following everyone out, felt a sense of betrayal. "I can't believe this," he muttered to himself, shaking his head in shock.

Chapter 22

REALIZATION

The small Thai restaurant nestled by a rocky outcrop on the beach exuded a cozy, rustic charm. Several lanterns, their soft glow casting intricate shadows, hung from bamboo poles, lending an enchanting ambiance to the location.

Seated at one of the weathered wooden tables were Anthony and Harry, a basket of steaming jasmine rice between them. The aroma of Thai spices and grilled seafood lingered enticingly in the air.

"So, Harry, how did you get the police to come to the hospital?" Anthony asked, still confused about what he had witnessed earlier that day.

"I asked Nop to do it. You see, as we were waiting for the ambulance, it became clear to me that Marieke had disengaged my brakes. She specifically set that scooter aside for me and made a point of it before we set off," Harry explained. "When Nop came back with the ambulance, I shared with him my suspicion. He was quite shocked and agreed with me that we should inform the police. His reasoning was that if Clara pressed charges, an innocent employee from the retreat might go to prison for causing bodily harm due to negligence."

"I can imagine that happening. He was right to inform the authorities before Marieke invented a bunch of lies to cover up her tracks."

"I agree, but I never imagined that Marieke would also confess to trying to kill James. She must have felt cornered, believing we were near uncovering the truth, and decided to take the blame for both crimes."

"But why did she want to silence you? I thought Marieke was the one who sought your help to investigate James's supposed accident."

Harry nodded, her gaze holding the flickering candlelight. "That's right! Something changed in the last few days. She must have found out who tried to kill James. And if that is so, the only person she would go to such lengths to protect is her wife, isn't it?"

Anthony's eyes widened as he sought to grasp the unfolding drama. "Yvonne? But I thought Marieke confessed to it?"

Harry sighed, her fingers tracing an invisible pattern on the table's surface. "It's complex, Anthony. I believe she confessed to protect the real killer, Yvonne."

Anthony's disbelief was palpable. "Why in the world would she do that?"

Harry's voice lowered, her eyes clouded with a tinge of sadness. "Because of Yvonne's past. Yvonne spent over a decade in a Thai prison for smuggling cocaine—an experience that left her broken. She was given a life sentence but left prison on some kind of royal amnesty decree. However, if she gets arrested again, she'll be sent right back."

Anthony's confusion deepened as he sought to unravel the motives. "So, Marieke's parents didn't actually lose everything to James's investment company?" he inquired.

Harry shook her head, her expression contemplative. "No, that part of the story seems fabricated. I think Marieke came up with it on the spot, perhaps drawing from your own experience when you shared with us your story about how investment bankers had cost you your life's savings."

Anthony frowned, absorbing the revelation. "So, if it's not about James's current profession, then what's it really about?"

Harry lowered her voice as if sharing a secret. "I don't know, but I'm sure it's about James's past. There's something in his history, something he did or was involved in. I think he and Yvonne met before. I can't figure out how and when."

Their conversation was punctuated by the clinking of cutlery and soft chatter from the other diners in the restaurant. Amidst the fragrant aroma of Thai spices, the elderly owner of the restaurant approached their table.

"Is everything all right?" she inquired in English.

Harry offered a warm smile. "Oh, everything is perfect, as always. Your food is amazing, and we're enjoying every bite."

The Thai woman's lined face creased into a smile. "Thank you, dear."

Before she could walk away, Harry politely enquired, "By the way, has there been any news of Captain Lamai?"

Concern darkened the woman's eyes. "Nothing. We're all so worried. The whole community has been looking for her—we put posters all over the island and near the tourist spots, but we've heard nothing. It's as if she disappeared from the face of the earth. One minute she was on her boat, and the next, she was gone. It does not make any sense. Who would want to harm her?"

As the woman's words hung in the air, Harry's eyes widened with realization. She swiftly apologized to the owner and asked for the bill. "Oh my god! Anthony! I know how Marieke figured out it was Yvonne. The sarong! The black sarong that I found by the jetty the morning after Captain Lamai disappeared. It wasn't Amaya's. It was Yvonne's. Marieke must have recognized it then on the beach when I showed it to everybody. She must have checked at home if Yvonne still had it. That's how she knew Yvonne was involved. We need to hurry!"

Without wasting a moment, they dashed out of the restaurant and headed back to the retreat towards Yvonne and Marieke's house.

Chapter 23

THE TRUTH

Amidst the moon's silver glow, Anthony struggled to match Harry's rapid pace as they navigated the serpentine pathways. Their journey concluded at a colonial-style villa nestled toward the rear of the retreat—an exquisite building set on a gentle slope overlooking the bay. Although darkness veiled the surroundings, the villa's warm, inviting lights radiated from its interior through the windows.

Surrounded by enormous banana trees and ancient coconut palms that guarded the house, the old building stood as a silent sentinel over the tranquil bay. The architectural grandeur of the villa was unmistakable, with its arched windows that gleamed like pearls against the soft hues of the night. Through the expansive, open French windows at the front of the house, Harry and Anthony could witness Yvonne's frantic movements. Her silhouette darted from room to room, creating an atmosphere of palpable tension. She was packing her clothes and precious belongings, evaluating what to take and what to leave behind.

Harry ascended the veranda's steps and approached the open window. Yvonne, taken aback by Harry's unexpected presence, momentarily halted her actions. Their eyes locked for a suspended breath before Yvonne resumed her rapid packing in the bedroom.

"Yvonne, please, we need to talk," Harry called out gently.

Yvonne, her back turned, continued packing without acknowledging Harry's plea. Instead, she muttered, as much to herself as anyone, "I'm glad it's all over. I could not spend another minute in the company of that stupid cow, Lisa," she seethed, her words laced with bitterness. "For the last few days, I have been keeping her company. All she did was moan about her life and pity herself. Saying over and over that her life was destroyed. I could not take it anymore. What about my life? I spent almost a damn decade rotting away in that hellhole they call women's prison."

She paused, her memories hauntingly vivid.

"You can't even imagine what it was like. They treated us like animals in there," Yvonne continued, her voice cracking. "Imagine 60 women in one cell with two buckets for a toilet! The stench will haunt me forever. The constant chatter and cries. The gangs. I had to fight for every little thing I owned; the thin mat I slept on and the rags I was wearing. Disease was widespread, as they fed us slop that only made us sick. There was no one to ask for help; the guards thought they could do whatever they pleased—you have no idea what I saw. And then the endless hours of forced labor breaking our spirits, day by day."

Yvonne's hands clenched into fists; her knuckles white with tension.

"They don't care if you're innocent or guilty. Once you're inside, you're just a number," she hissed. "I watched women wither away from sickness, their pleas for medical help ignored. It was a living nightmare, and I swore I'd never go back."

She glanced over her shoulder at Harry and Anthony, her eyes a turbulent sea of anguish and fury.

Harry, filled with sympathy for Yvonne's torment, gently urged her to sit down and momentarily set her packing aside. Anthony, his expression a mix of curiosity and concern, couldn't hold back his question any longer.

"Yvonne," he began cautiously, "did James have any involvement in what happened to you in your arrest and imprisonment?"

Yvonne, her face etched with stress and worry, sank into an old rattan armchair. She placed a trembling hand on her forehead, as if trying to hold back a tide of painful memories.

"When he and Lisa arrived at the retreat," Yvonne said, her voice quivering with the weight of her past, "I didn't recognize him at first. It has been well over twenty years. He was a different man back then; slim, with long hair and a beard, and such a carefree spirit. But it was his voice, you see. When I heard it, everything came rushing back like a tidal wave."

She paused. The memories that she had tried to repress for the last two decades resurfaced with a vengeance.

"It was James who had me arrested and then left me alone to face the Thai judicial system," Yvonne continued, her voice barely above a whisper. "He's the one who planted cocaine in my suitcase. Him or one of his associates. I don't really know. The police at the Bangkok airport found drugs sewn into the underlining of my suitcase, but it wasn't even my suitcase. James gave it to me the day before our flight. We were going to fly from Thailand to the US to meet his parents, you see. I was convinced he was going to propose there."

"We met a month earlier in a bar in Phuket, and I fell for him instantly," she continued. "We spent a romantic month there. James was renting a small villa, and during that time, I was convinced I was living in paradise. I started planning our future together; you know, the kind of dreams you have when you're young and in love. I didn't see any warning signs, even though I should have. How can a twenty-something-year-old afford to rent a villa? He'd disappear for days at a time, and never told me where he went or what he did. He never told me what he did for a living. There were many question marks, but I was foolishly in love and ignored them."

"When James announced that we should go to the United States to visit his family, I was over the moon. In my mind, I was envisioning my new life in the States. I was imagining the proposal: in front of his parents after a nice dinner, he'd go down on one knee and present me with a diamond ring. We'd start a life together."

As Yvonne continued to share the events that had led to her arrest, her anger toward James grew with every word she spoke. The resentment that had simmered within her for decades began to surface.

"But it never happened," she went on, her voice breaking. "When we arrived at the airport in Bangkok, James told me to go ahead and wait in the check-in line. He complained that he had a stomachache and said he needed to use the restroom. He assured me he'd catch up with me in a few minutes. As I stood in line with my suitcase on the trolley, an airport security officer walked by with a sniffer dog. The dog went crazy when he smelled my bags. I was asked to leave the line and follow the security officer. They searched my bags and found the bricks of cocaine."

"So, James used you as a sort of decoy," Anthony suggested.

Yvonne nodded vigorously. "That's exactly what happened. He must have been watching from a distance. I believe it was he who informed the security officers of the possible smuggling attempt. Once the officers were busy searching my bags and collecting evidence against me, other mules must have slipped through."

Anthony's eyes widened as the implications became clearer. "He might have had other young women transporting drugs on that same day. Your arrest could have been the distraction they needed. It might also have been a kind of a bribe for the airport security—I'm sure they get rewarded when they catch smugglers."

Yvonne nodded again, her eyes welling up with tears at the memory. "I think that's how the gang operated. They would send a few girls traveling at the same time, and some would make it through while others got caught."

Harry couldn't help but wonder aloud, "But why didn't the police actively search for him? Didn't you tell them about the setup?"

Yvonne sighed deeply. "At first, I had no idea what was going on. I thought it was a mistake. I couldn't believe that it was happening to me. By the time I got put in jail, James had vanished. I kept telling the detective to get him, but it was as if James had never existed. My plane ticket was purchased only in my name and it was bought with cash at a small travel office in Phuket. Once I started to look through my photos, I realized that I didn't have a single photograph of him." She paused, the weight of her story bearing down on her. "Whenever we were taking photos, he would end up out of the shot, or hidden behind a tree, or obscured by someone else's head. It was not until the police asked me for his photo that I realized what he had been doing."

"But the police must have known that you were a victim in this," Harry said.

"I'm sure they knew. I wasn't the first or the last young woman duped like that. But they didn't care. They treated me as if I deserved this. Like it was my fault for being stupid. And to be honest, for many years, I felt like this myself. I blamed myself. I lost all my self-esteem. I was nothing. It took me a long time to rebuild who I am. To bring back the trusting and fun-loving Yvonne. Then, when I've finally put my life back together again, he appears out of nowhere. Oblivious to who I was. As if I was nothing. Every comment he and Lisa made about their wonderful lives, their beautiful children..." Yvonne's words trailed off, overcome by a tidal wave of emotion.

"You see, I can't have children. I developed an infection while I was in prison," Yvonne explained coldly, as if talking about someone else's experience. "It went untreated for months, and by the time they intervened, it was too late. They had to perform a hysterectomy to save my life." Her voice quivered as she recounted the injustice she had endured.

"The prison took everything from me: my identity, my youth, my hope for a family of my own... They stripped away my future, my chance to have the love and happiness that James and his kind take for granted."

Her voice filled with anger and sorrow. "Seeing him living his life after he has destroyed so many others... It sickened me to my core."

"Are you sure he did it to other women?" Harry asked.

Yvonne, her voice steady now, began to reveal a broader scope of deception. "I wasn't the only one who fell victim to James and his gang," she explained. "During my time in prison, I met other women who had been tricked by them. These women were all young and vulnerable; not just Europeans, but also young Thai women who had dreams of a better life."

Her story continued to unfold. "I met another Dutch woman who had been in prison before my arrival. She told me the truth about James. She met him in Amsterdam when she was only nineteen. James seemed like a typical American backpacker, and he suggested they go to Thailand together. She thought it was a romantic gateway. They stayed in Phuket, and, like me, she was arrested in Bangkok with a suitcase laced with cocaine."

The trio sat in the dimly lit room, the weight of the past hanging heavily in the air.

Anthony leaned forward, concern etched on his face. "Do you think Lisa knows about James's past?" he asked Yvonne.

Yvonne shook her head slowly. "I'm not sure. I never saw her around when we lived in Phuket together, but she might have been hiding. It might be why he would go away for days at a time and not explain to me where he'd been."

As Yvonne spoke, Harry's eyes seemed to light up with a revelation. "Clara mentioned that when her parents were young, they used to backpack around the world," she said. "Lisa must have known about the drugs. In fact, Lisa might have been the one pulling the strings, the real gang leader, while James lured these young women into his trap."

"It's possible, and I'm sure they're doing it again. I overheard them telling someone how they were touring Asia—they were planning to go to Malaysia and Vietnam. These are all drug smuggling routes. They're back, making money and destroying lives."

As Yvonne spoke, Harry wondered if this was the source of money that James was bragging about when she had spoken to him at the Emerald Lake.

"I had to stop him," Yvonne said, trying to justify her actions. "I had a plan to make it look like an accident—a falling coconut was supposed to be a perfect crime. I hid a heavy hammer not far from where I was going to set my yoga mat during the mindfulness session. To make sure James left the session and walked under the coconut palms, I served him a strong laxative. Do you remember the detox cocktails that I brought to the jetty when you came back from the boat trip? Well, James's was marked. I made sure he finished it. Then, during the mindfulness session, I saw him stand up and walk away. I sneaked behind and hit him hard. He didn't see it coming. He fell instantly. I took a moment to look him in the face before he passed out. I think he recognized me because he said my name before his eyes closed. Then I ran back to the beach."

While Yvonne's motives were clear, Harry still had many questions that had to be answered. *How was it possible that no one saw her leave the session?* However, a more urgent matter was at hand, which was the main reason why she and Anthony had rushed to the villa.

"Yvonne!" Harry spoke in a somber tone. "What happened to Lamai? Where is she?"

"I'm so sorry about Lamai," Yvonne said, starting to sob. The weight of her guilt was unbearable. "I'm so sorry. I did it to save lives, and then I killed an innocent person. I should have sought justice the right way, not taken matters into my own hands." She choked with regret. "But I didn't think anyone would believe me that James was a drug dealer. I wanted to avenge myself, my younger self. And now Lamai is dead."

Harry's eyes widened in shock. "Dead?" she repeated, her voice a mixture of horror and disbelief. "Yvonne, what have you done?"

Yvonne's trembling hands betrayed her guilt as she nodded slowly. "After the attack, I had hidden the hammer under some banana leaves. I was going to come back for it later. It was late at night after the storm when I went to look for it. That's when I saw Marieke with a torch searching the area. The wind during the storm must have blown away the leaves because she found it quite quickly. My silly wife took the hammer home," she explained, distinct sadness in her tone. "I couldn't believe it. My meticulously orchestrated plan was falling apart because of the one person that I wanted to protect. I followed her and watched her from outside. She wrapped the hammer in a bag and hid it in our bedroom. It did not take me long the next morning to find it in a shoe box inside our closet. Can you imagine what would have happened if the police had decided to investigate James's accident? If they found that hammer with his blood in our bedroom, they'd send us both to jail. I took the hammer and, at night, went to the end of the jetty to toss it into the sea. But Lamai saw me..."

Harry's face paled as she grasped the enormity of Yvonne's revelation. The consequences of Yvonne's actions were now far more severe than she had imagined.

Yvonne's voice trembled as she recounted the events that had transpired on that fateful night on the jetty. "When I heard Lamai's voice, everything changed. She recognized me." Yvonne's words were filled with guilt. "I realized she must have seen the bloodied hammer. I panicked. I walked back to the beach where she was sitting, and before she could say anything, I... I struck her on the head with a stone. She fell unconscious."

Harry listened in stunned silence. "I decided to hide her body in the cave not far from the jetty," she admitted, her voice quivering. "I don't know what came over me. I had to drag her along the beach and then pull her through a small opening between the water's surface and the cave. The tide was very low, so I managed to do it, but since then, the entrance has been almost inaccessible."

"I found some fishing ropes on the beach, among the driftwood, and tied her up before I left," Yvonne added. "I'm so sorry. I really don't understand why I did it."

Harry reached into her satchel and retrieved the black sarong. She held it up for Yvonne to see. "Is this yours?" Harry asked.

Yvonne nodded, her eyes filled with remorse.

"Yes, I put it over my head in case someone saw me, but then I lost it on the way to the cave. I couldn't find it among the mangroves."

"That's how Marieke knew it was you," Harry told Yvonne. "She identified your sarong. Then, to confirm her suspicion, she must have checked if the hammer was still hidden in your bedroom. Once she saw the empty shoe box, her thought was confirmed. That's why she tried to stop me, to protect *you*."

"Are you going to call the police?" Yvonne asked, trembling. "I...I can't go back to prison."

"There's no time," Harry said urgently. "We need to check if Lamai is still in that cave. What if she is still alive? If we don't get her out tonight, the high tide will make it impossible."

"We need to act fast," Anthony agreed. "But how are we going to access the cave? The entrance is probably below the sea level already."

"I don't know, Anthony, but I can't sit here and do nothing. We must at least try."

"Can you dive?" A plan was hatching in Anthony's mind.

"I can snorkel, but diving is beyond my abilities. And I'm not a strong swimmer."

"Then we need Euclid," Anthony said decisively. "He's just completed his PADI course."

As they rushed outside, Yvonne stayed behind. Harry was certain that she'd never see her again, but there was no time. It would take a few hours to get through to an English-speaking detective and explain the case. In Harry's mind, saving Lamai was more important. The high tide was reaching its momentum and if there was any hope that the captain would still be alive, they had to act fast.

Chapter 24

Last Moments

Trapped in the darkness of the cave, with the rising tide again creeping steadily upward, and with her hands and feet still tightly bound, Lamai felt a profound sense of dread. She had been stuck within these suffocating confines for two days now; her only companions being the eerie echoes of her own thoughts and the filthy bats that swooped in and out of the cave through a small opening higher up in the cliff face. Fear gnawed at her heart, and the chill of the rising water almost touching her chin again proved a cruel reminder of her precarious situation on the elevated rock shelf at the back of the cave. Over the past two days, she had experienced four high tides inside the cave. Each time, most of her body but her face was submerged by the cold, dark waters that rushed into the cave for a period of one hour. She did not know how much more of this torture she could take.

As she faced what she believed might be her final moments, Lamai's exhausted mind drifted back to a cherished memory from her childhood—that of a perfect day, untouched by the cold, watery fingers that now enveloped her.

In that distant recollection, Lamai was a carefree child of seven or eight, visiting her grandparents' rice farm in the lush northern countryside of Thailand. It was a time when the entire family, along with neighbors and relatives, toiled tirelessly in the fields during the busy harvest season. But on this particular day, young Lamai had decided to embark on a special mission of preparing a meal for everyone, a small act that would forever be etched in her memory.

In her imagination, she saw herself gathering the ingredients from the bustling kitchen of her grandparents' humble home. The dish she had chosen to make was a simple yet beloved Thai farmer's meal—Pad Kra Pao. With an innocence that only a child possessed, she set to work, her small hands confidently wielding a mortar and pestle to crush a generous handful of garlic and chilies. The fragrant aroma of fresh basil leaves filled the air as she plucked them from the family's vegetable garden, and the savory scent of minced pork sizzled in the wok she had carefully placed over the gas burner.

She cooked in secret, a mischievous smile on her face, stealing moments of delight as she imagined the surprise and joy she would bring to the weary laborers when they finished their work in the field. As the golden sun descended toward the horizon, casting a warm, orange glow across the farm, Lamai emerged from the kitchen with her culinary masterpiece served up in a large metal bowl with a lid that was clipped securely in place.

After carefully arranging the dish on a tray next to a pile of small plastic serving bowls, and with several spoons in her pocket, she ventured into the field nearby where the adults were just finishing their toil, their bodies weary from the day's labor. Their faces lit up with astonishment as they saw young Lamai approaching, bearing her precious gift—a feast of Pad Kra Pao, steaming rice, and slices of fresh cucumber.

Lamai remembered the laughter and camaraderie that had ensued; the sound of spoons clinking, and the shared moments of respite and joy at the end of their labor. It was a day of harmony, a testament to the simple pleasures of life. Lamai's memory of the radiant smile on her grandparents' faces remained imprinted in her heart.

As Lamai's desperate struggle against the encroaching water continued, she clung fervently to the memories of that blissful evening in the rice field. In her mind's eye, she had transported herself back to that treasured moment. Then something incredible happened. Her cold, trembling body ceased to exist, and she returned to the farm, surrounded by the sights, sounds, and scents of that blissful evening.

She felt the warmth of the golden hour's gentle radiance as the sun painted the world of her childhood in hues of orange and gold. Standing in the midst of the rice field, she saw herself with her beloved grandmother, sharing a meal that her young, innocent hands had lovingly prepared. They laughed together, their hearts light and free, amid the tranquil expanse of the countryside.

The enticing aroma of her favorite childhood dish filled the air, mingling with the fragrant basil leaves. Lamai watched in her mind's eye as her grandmother, a figure of wisdom and love, took a bite of her dish. Her face lit up with delight, and her voice, rich with the warmth of approval, proclaimed it the best Pad Kra Pao she had ever tasted.

During this immersive, out-of-body experience, Lamai felt her senses come alive. She experienced the texture of the freshly cooked rice in her mouth as she savored each spoonful. The grains gave her comfort and nourishment. Laughter filled her ears, accompanied by a chorus of joyous voices that somehow blended with the sound of water moving irresistibly over rocks toward her.

Suddenly, a soft presence brushed against her legs, and Lamai glanced down to find the figure of Raam, her ginger kitten, weaving affectionately around her legs. A rush of affection and reassurance washed over her. She hoped in that fleeting moment that her grandmother was taking care of Raam just as she had taken care of her in life.

But then, as Lamai's consciousness waxed and waned between delirium and confusion, the frigid waters of the cave again reached out for her. Lamai's mind grew dark and heavy. The vivid recollection she had just experienced, including all the laughter and the love, slipped away, leaving her cold and adrift once more. Sharp rocks pushed into her back and side, yet, in her heart, the imprint of that perfect day remained in the face of impending darkness.

Chapter 25

The Rescue

With only the moon to light them, Harry, Anthony, and Euclid gathered by the shore, their faces etched with determination and concern.

"I can't swim into the cave in the dark. I must take the torch with me," Euclid explained, looking at the spot towards where the cave's entrance should be.

"It's incredible how high the tide is tonight. A few days ago, anyone could have walked there. Now, it's like it was never there," Anthony added.

Euclid nodded, deeply troubled. "And those waves are pounding the rocks around the bay. It's too risky."

Harry, always quick to think on her feet, asked, "Would it help if we had a boat?"

"Yes, we could use it to carry ropes and lifejackets closer to the mouth of the cave. But we can't waste too much time," Euclid explained.

"We'll get Lamai's crew to bring the boat and equipment while you start swimming toward the cave, Euclid," Harry said. "The boat will be there to help pull Lamai out of the water."

Euclid nodded, his resolve firm. "Sounds like a good plan. Let's get moving." With that, he took a deep breath, preparing himself for the challenging swim to rescue Lamai from her maritime prison.

As the moonlight glistened across the turbulent sea, Euclid, clad in his scuba gear, bravely leaped into the waves. He began his swim toward the cave where Lamai was trapped, determination guiding his every stroke.

"What if it's too late?" Anthony looked at Harry. "It's quite possible that Yvonne's blow killed her or that she drowned afterward and was left tied up in the cave."

"I don't want to even consider that," Harry replied stubbornly, her determination infectious. "We must try. If she's still alive, it's her last chance to be rescued. By the morning, the water will have completely filled the cave."

"Are you sure about that?" Anthony asked.

"I've heard someone ask Lamai's crew about tides when we were on her boat," Harry spoke rapidly. "I remember them talking about the approaching spring tide—it's the highest tide of the month. They said that most of the caves on the coast get completely submerged at that time."

With this said, Harry and Anthony sprinted toward the jetty, their hearts pounding with a mixture of hope and fear. They reached the boat, and Preecha emerged from the deck below, looking bewildered. He inquired urgently about the situation, but Harry, breathless and anxious, cut him off.

"No time to explain," Harry gasped. "We need to save Captain Lamai. She's trapped in the cave around the corner." She pointed toward the ominous opening in the cliffs.

"How will we get her out of the cave at full tide?" Preecha asked, unsure of the rescue plan.

"Euclid is already on his way with scuba gear. He'll dive in through the submerged opening to reach her," Anthony replied resolutely.

Realizing that time was of the essence, Preecha didn't press for further details. He swiftly called out to another crew member, barking directions in rapid Thai. Anthony joined him to help untie the boat while Harry took a seat at the front, her eyes focused on guiding them to the mouth of the cave, hoping that Lamai was still alive.

As the boat's searchlight cut across the dark waters, they soon spotted Euclid's head bobbing among the waves near the mouth of the cave. Preecha skillfully directed the searchlight toward where the waves were crashing against the rocks surrounding the submerged opening.

Preecha quickly made a call on the radio, communicating at length with someone. "I've just contacted the Coast Guard for assistance. They'll be here soon. They're always on standby for rescue missions. You really should have contacted them first before Euclid set off," he explained, putting the radio microphone in its holder.

"I'm sorry. We had to act fast and I didn't think of that," Harry admitted her mistake. "How long will it take them to get here?"

"Not very long; they'll be here shortly. They don't waste time in emergencies," Preecha reassured her.

Euclid swam to the side of the boat, and Preecha explained to him that the Coast Guard would be on site soon. The men had to holler in order to be heard over the crashing waves. With a thumbs-up, Euclid indicated that he was ready to continue with the rescue and head for the cave opening, just twenty meters away. The boat could not get any closer because the breaking waves and the current would push it against the rocks. Just as Euclid was about to dive in, Preecha realized that their plan was not complete.

"You'll need another mask if she's still alive," he shouted over the waves. He reached into a box containing the guests' diving equipment and retrieved a snorkel mask. "For whatever it's worth," he added, passing it to Euclid, who secured the mask by its rubber strap to his arm before disappearing beneath the surface of the water.

Euclid found himself submerged in the dark, tropical waters of Koh Samui, surrounded by an eerie silence only broken by the turbulent rumble of the breaking waves and his controlled breathing. The torch that was attached to the top of his mask created a sharp tunnel of light before him. Whatever direction he turned his head, the light beam followed, illuminating the water and reflecting off thousands of particles in the water. Startled fish swam quickly toward the light, only to become disorientated once they passed Euclid's head and suddenly found themselves once again in darkness. It was a surreal experience, one that Euclid had dreamt of when he did the training for his PADI certificate. But now, the circumstances were far from the tranquil, relaxed dives he'd imagined he would make. This was his first solo night dive, and to top it all, he had to locate a missing person in a submerged cave.

Euclid scanned the underwater landscape, the torchlight casting strange silhouettes on the sand and rocks that covered the sea floor. The coral reef, usually vibrant with color during the day, now appeared ghostly and ethereal in the dim light. The wetsuit he was wearing embraced him like a comfort blanket. He swam forward with strong, confident strokes of his flippers and entered the narrow opening of the cave. Sharp rock surrounded him on both sides, and he looked up to see bubbles and froth floating above him on the surface of a rocky ceiling. The cave floor rose before him as he penetrated the dark recess of the cave. There! Right in front of him, he spotted a dark, twisted shape ahead, partially concealed by a semi-submerged rock shelf. His heart raced as he approached, realizing that he had found what he was looking for. He had found Lamai's body motionless in the water.

A cold feeling of dread settled across his heart as Euclid reached for his diving belt, his fingers searching for his knife with which he could cut the ropes that bound her. Panic flickered as he realized he hadn't packed it. In his rush to gather his diving equipment, he had not thought of how useful a knife might be.

Fear and urgency coursed through his mind. There was no time to swim back to the boat; Lamai depended on him. He clenched his fists in frustration and crouched over her body to assess the situation, his mind racing.

Euclid touched Lamai gently, lifting her head above the level of the restless water. His heart leaped with relief as Lamai opened her eyes briefly and moaned gently; a glimmer of consciousness. It was clear that she was disoriented and in pain.

Swiftly, Euclid submerged his head and trained the torchlight across Lamai's recumbent body. With utmost care, he began to work on the knots. The rope, swelled by the seawater, resisted his efforts. However, Euclid's determination matched the urgency of the situation. He pulled and pried the knots open, loosening them inch-by-inch, and eventually he freed Lamai's poor, swollen hands.

Now, Lamai's eyes were wide open. She tried to speak, but her voice was shaky and terribly creaky.

Euclid nodded, and although his diving equipment prevented him from speaking clearly, his concerned eyes conveyed reassurance. He gestured for her to hold on to him, signaling that it was time to return to the beach outside the submerged cave. Lamai nodded weakly, her trust in this newfound underwater savior evident in how she clung to him.

Together, they traversed the water, and a quick dive below the surface at the mouth of the cave would see them free from the nightmare that had taken place within its depths.

Euclid's heart soared with relief as Lamai signaled her understanding and readiness to make the dive. He quickly handed her the extra diving mask he had strapped to his arm and offered her the scuba tank's mouthpiece. Lamai inserted the device into her mouth and took a deep breath.

After taking a gulp of air at the surface, Euclid dove under the water with Lamai, guiding her under the rocky overhang that concealed their exit. The cave's oppressive darkness gave way to the welcoming sight of the moonlit waters outside.

They were greeted by the radiance of a powerful rescue light. The Coast Guard's boat was waiting for them, its crew poised for action. As soon as they spotted Lamai and Euclid, the rescuers leaped into the water, assisting Lamai onto a stretcher they had prepared at the stern of the Coast Guard motorboat.

The Coast Guard paramedics went to work immediately, checking Lamai's vital signs and monitoring her condition. They assessed the injuries she had suffered during her ordeal in the cave and gave her oxygen to breathe. Since she was so dehydrated, they then inserted an IV line in her arm.

With Lamai in capable hands and beginning to stabilize, the captain of the Coast Guard boat increased the speed of the engines, causing the vessel to surge forward. They were now racing toward the nearest hospital to provide Lamai with the medical attention she so urgently needed. Euclid, Harry, and Anthony remained with Preecha on the small tour boat, relieved and hoping for Lamai's recovery.

CHAPTER 26

COCKTAILS FOR EVERYONE

The group gathered at the beach bar the following day. Anthony stepped forward, raising his hand to signal the bartender.

"Let's celebrate," he declared with a grin. "Cocktails for everyone!"

Clinking glasses and joyful cheers followed as they toasted Euclid's incredible rescue mission.

"Thank you," Euclid said, blushing. "But it was really Harry and Anthony who saved her. If they didn't insist on checking that cave in the middle of the night, Lamai would have... you know... the tide was very high last night."

"Humble as always," Sarah said, giving Euclid a warm embrace. "That's why I love you."

"To Harry and Anthony!" everyone cheered.

Amaya's curiosity got the best of her, and she asked the question that was on everyone's mind. "So, does anyone have any news about Yvonne? Was she arrested last night?"

Anthony took a sip of his cocktail before filling them in on the latest developments. "Well, after Lamai was taken to hospital, we asked Preecha to call the police and explain about the attempted murders of her and James. The police were very concerned with the abduction of the captain. When the police showed up at Yvonne and Marieke's villa last night, Yvonne had already vanished."

"Vanished?" Amaya raised an eyebrow.

"She left behind a short letter apologizing to Lamai and her family. Yvonne claimed she wasn't herself during the attack and that she deeply regretted it," Harry added more context to the situation.

"But here's the kicker. In the same letter, Yvonne said she had no regrets about what she did to James. She believed he got what he deserved," Anthony continued.

The group fell into a heavy silence, the weight of this revelation settling in.

Harry then broke the quiet tension with another piece of intriguing information. "Oh, and the letter was signed 'Moira'."

"Moira? Who's Moira?" Mary asked, somewhat confused.

"As it turns out, *Moira* is actually Yvonne's real name. When the police searched the house, they found her old Dutch passport and some court documents about her trial from the time before she changed her identity. Her name was Moira de Kruijff, but she changed her first name to Yvonne once she left prison. She was trying to leave her past behind," Harry said, sharing the surprising revelation.

The group exchanged glances, their thoughts drifting to the enigmatic woman who had woven her tragic story into their own lives but had left them with more questions than answers.

Mary's voice held a touch of melancholy as she contemplated the name Moira. "Moira... it means 'fate' or 'destiny', doesn't it? Was it Yvonne's destiny to never find happiness?"

She shook her head, her expression filled with sorrow. "It's just so sad that she came here, to this beautiful island, hoping for a fresh start. But it all unraveled."

Harry nodded, her gaze distant. "You know, it's strange. All of this started with her wife trying to figure out what had happened to James in order to keep the retreat safe."

Perplexed, the others exchanged curious glances. Amaya voiced their shared confusion, asking, "What do you mean, Harry?"

Harry recounted the night of James's accident, when Marieke had approached her with suspicions of foul play. "Marieke believed that what happened to James wasn't an accident. She thought someone had tried to kill him."

"Why would she think that?" Mary asked.

"She found a bloodied hammer near the place where James was found unconscious," Harry explained further. "I think because of Yvonne's traumatic past, Marieke didn't want to burden her wife with the worry that there might be a killer among the retreat's guests. She confided in me, hoping that I could help her catch whoever had tried to murder James. Little did she know that she set in motion events that would unravel her whole life and marriage."

The group absorbed this revelation.

"But how did Yvonne attack James? We were all there watching her," Mary said, struggling to comprehend how Yvonne had tried to murder James during the mindfulness session. Her confusion mirrored that of the others, and they turned to Harry, seeking clarification.

Harry explained, her voice tinged with an air of mystery. "That was something that puzzled me for a long time as well," she admitted. "But then, early this morning, Anthony, Euclid, Sarah, and I decided to recreate the session at the same spot we were at when James was assaulted."

Everyone listened intently, eager to understand what had transpired.

Harry continued, "If you recall, during the original session, we weren't really looking at Yvonne. We were all facing the sea, deeply immersed in our meditation, mentally tuning into the waves and the soothing sounds of the ocean. Yvonne was sitting behind us and had effectively managed to hypnotize us. Our eyes were closed, and we were all focused on our personal mantras."

"But how would she hypnotize us? Don't you need to be a professional hypnotist to do that?" Amaya asked, surprised.

"When Yvonne confessed that it was her who tried to kill James, I couldn't stop thinking about everything that Marieke had told me about her wife's past. That's when I remembered her telling me that, after she was released from prison, Yvonne did several courses in alternative therapies. I thought she had mentioned hypnotherapy, among many others. To confirm that, I started to search the internet," Harry explained. "Something I should have done from the start. She used to work on cruise ships, so I had to dig deep and search expat newspapers and social media groups. I checked the websites of all the cruise companies that operate in Thailand. It took me a while, but I stumbled upon an article from a cruise ship newsletter that hailed Yvonne de Kruijff as their best hypnotherapist."

This information hung in the air, the last piece of the puzzle that slowly slid into place.

Harry continued, "With us hypnotized and in deep meditation, she only had to disappear for a few minutes. Once we heard Marieke's scream, we all ran to her. But I can't even remember whether Yvonne was with us or not."

Anthony nodded slowly. "That's true. I can't truly testify to whether Yvonne was with us or not. I assumed she was."

"Sounds like a classic case of misdirection," Euclid explained. "You know, inducing selective attention for a group of people. I've read psychology articles about this. Apparently, people can miss something as obvious as a gorilla walking through a basketball game if they have been tasked to count the number of ball passes between the players."

Sarah chimed in, "Oh, I know about that. It's called the 'invisible gorilla experiment'. It proves how our brains can overlook something unexpected when we're hyper-focused on one task."

Harry grinned. "Exactly like how Yvonne manipulated our attention during the mindfulness session. While we were in deep meditation, she simply disappeared for those crucial minutes. When we heard Marieke's cries for help, we all rushed to help her, none of us recalling whether Yvonne was with us or not."

Anthony added, "It was like a magician's trick—distract your audience, and they won't see the sleight of hand."

"So, she created the perfect illusion, making James's 'accident' appear like a magic trick while we were the unsuspecting audience who was supposed to give her an alibi," Amaya said.

Harry nodded and smiled knowingly. "Precisely."

Mary sipped her cocktail, reflecting on all the information; her eyes fixed on the waves crashing along the shore.

"Wait a second," she said suddenly, a look of realization washing over her face. "Something's still not clear. Yvonne was behind James's accident, but what about Clara? Why did Marieke try to kill her?"

Harry set down her drink. "Ah, yes. Let's not forget Marieke, who's currently in jail for that particular attempted murder. She did try to kill me, whether she feels remorseful about it or not."

"I remember she was oddly specific about who should ride which scooter. I thought it was just her being her usual organized self," Sarah added. "You know, micromanaging."

Harry agreed. "That's what I thought initially. But then, as Fate would have it, Clara ended up taking my scooter by mistake on the way back from the elephant sanctuary."

"So, Marieke tampered with what she thought would be your scooter. That's... that's just evil," Mary said.

Harry sighed. "Yes. After I showed her the black sarong that I had found among the mangroves, Marieke must have realized that it was Yvonne who had tried to kill James. But instead of confronting her wife about it, she took matters into her own hands and tried to put things straight by getting rid of me. It's almost like a comedy of errors if it weren't so tragic."

"This retreat was supposed to be a safe haven. A place for rest and spiritual growth. Instead, it turned into a battleground for revenge," Mary reflected. "It shows you that no matter how much we try to hide our past, it has a way of catching up with us."

Sarah nodded in agreement. "Especially since taking matters into our own hands can hurt innocent people. Yvonne had wanted revenge against James, but it ruined her marriage and sent her wife to jail. Where do you think she's gone?"

"She must have taken a boat to mainland Thailand by now. From there, she could easily disappear into Laos or Malaysia," Anthony speculated. "If she changes her name again, she could easily blend in as a yoga instructor in a small resort in the middle of nowhere. Another new beginning."

"It's very sad," Harry commented. "I can sort of understand Yvonne's anger at James. He tricked young women into smuggling drugs for him and destroyed dozens of lives. He should face punishment, too, and not just because of what he did to Yvonne. And let's not forget Lisa; she also seems to be complicit in all this. From what Clara told us about her parents' globetrotting youth, I strongly suspect that Lisa was involved."

"It would be very hard to prove anything after all these years. Both James and Lisa seem to have reinvented themselves. They've become law-abiding middle-class citizens," Amaya observed. "A perfect suburban couple."

"I've been thinking about this since Yvonne told me her story last night." Harry's voice dropped to a hushed tone. "She thought that James and Lisa were planning to re-resume their drug smuggling venture. Now that their children have left home, it would make sense. But we need solid evidence that would stand up in court. And to get that, I need your help to set up a trap."

"What kind of trap are we talking about?" Euclid asked, looking intrigued.

Harry outlined her plan.

Chapter 27

THE TRAP

Mary walked briskly through the gardens of the yoga retreat, her steps uneven on the sandy path. As usual, the morning on Koh Samui was stunning—birds chirped in the trees, and colorful flowers adorned the bushes. But Mary felt none of the island's tranquility. Her task was too important; it required all her concentration.

Harry had assigned her the mission, and her hands shook with a mix of anxiety and determination as she thought about it. "You can do this," she whispered to herself, clutching the smartphone in her pocket.

Taking deep breaths to steady herself, Mary thought of the young women whose lives had been ruined by James and Lisa's criminal activities. Women whose youth had been wasted in Thai prisons because they had been duped into smuggling drugs. Mary's anger simmered for those women; she, too, had once been young and free-spirited.

"How could anyone exploit such innocence?" she thought, feeling a wave of revulsion for people who took advantage of other people's trust and openness.

As Mary reached Lisa's hut, she hesitated, her heart pounding in her chest like a drum. "This is it," she thought. "No turning back now."

Summoning every ounce of false confidence she could muster, she knocked on the door with a sense of urgency that she hoped would mask her nervousness. Her hand trembled as her knuckles left the wooden surface, retreating back to her side. She felt beads of sweat forming on her forehead despite the morning's cool breeze. The few seconds waiting for the door to open stretched out like hours, and her mind raced with possibilities, each more frightening than the last.

Would Lisa see through her act? Would she sniff out the deception and confront her?

Mary took one last shaky breath, preparing herself for what lay on the other side of that door. The birdsong now seemed like a distant, irrelevant serenade.

Then she heard the slow and deliberate footsteps coming from inside the hut.

And the door began to creak open.

Lisa's door opened fully, revealing her puffy face and dark circles under her eyes. She looked as if she had been through an emotional storm.

"Lisa, you won't believe the news I just got from the hospital!" Mary blurted out, her voice filled with feigned urgency.

Lisa's eyes widened, alarmed. "Is it Clara? Is she alright?"

Mary interrupted her, her voice high-pitched and almost unnaturally cheerful. "No, no, it's not Clara. It's James! He's just woken up from his coma!"

Lisa's expression turned from disbelief to astonishment. She looked like she might fall, so Mary quickly extended an arm out for her to lean on. "Come on, let's sit you down," Mary urged, guiding Lisa back into the hut.

Once inside, Lisa collapsed onto a wicker chair, still in a state of shock. Mary continued to pour out her well-rehearsed story.

"The hospital called the retreat's reception desk—they couldn't get hold of your number. They said it was urgent. James has been asking for you."

Tears filled Lisa's eyes as she slowly absorbed the information. "I can't believe it," she whispered. "James woke up... My husband is awake."

Mary felt her stomach tighten at the sight of Lisa's tears. This was a woman who had wrecked countless lives, yet here she was, showing vulnerability and empathy at the thought of her husband's condition. *Could she have been involved in her husband's crimes?* A doubt crossed Mary's mind, but there was no room to retreat now.

"Would you like to call the hospital now? He's been asking specifically for you," Mary pressed on, careful to maintain her urgent tone.

Lisa nodded. Mary selected the number on her phone and passed it over, holding her breath as Lisa put the phone to her ear.

"I'll give you some privacy," Mary whispered and headed outside. It was crucial for Lisa to feel like she could speak freely. If the trap worked, they would have the evidence they needed to bring James and Lisa to justice. If it didn't, Mary wasn't sure what would happen next.

Inside the hut, Lisa waited until James's voice came through the phone: "Lisa?"

"Yes, it's me," Lisa began, unaware that each word she uttered might be her undoing. "James! I can't believe it! It's you, really! I was so worried."

At the Koh Samui police station, Harry and Euclid were on the edge of their seats. The Thai detectives watched on intently, the atmosphere thick with tension. Harry's phone was on speakerphone, and Lisa's voice was coming through clearly. Euclid held a finger hovering over his phone screen, ready to play the next prerecorded message from James. A police tape recorder on the table before them had been switched on.

"Lisa, I need to tell you something," James's voice continued. "Do you remember Moira? We met her in Phuket. She was supposed to take goods for us to the US. Do you remember?"

Lisa seemed unnerved by this line of questioning. "James, why are you talking about Moira? It's ancient history. That girl was an idiot, just like the others."

"I know. She got arrested before she even got on the plane. Did you set her up? It looked like the police knew she had the product in the suitcase. They brought the sniffer dogs as soon as she arrived at the check-in desk."

Lisa's terse voice emerged from the smartphone's speaker, tinged with annoyance and apprehension. "Why are you bringing this up, James? Those were mistakes of the past. Why are you digging them up? It would be best if you stopped talking. You had a concussion. It's affecting your head."

Euclid had his finger poised over the next voice message and was ready to play it. The room collectively held its breath. Would Lisa incriminate herself further? Would she take the bait?

James's voice again filled the room. "Lisa, we've done so much harm. I've been thinking maybe it's time to come clean. I can't live with the weight of this any longer. We've ruined lives, Lisa. Women fell to addiction or were caught and ended up in jail. I can't keep going like this."

For a moment, there was silence on the other end. Then Lisa's voice crackled through the speaker, thick with barely suppressed rage. "Shut up, James. Just shut up. You're being incredibly ungrateful."

Harry's eyes widened. She looked at the detectives, who were listening intently and taking notes.

Lisa continued, her voice seething with anger. "Do you have any idea what I've done for you? For us? I spent endless nights searching for girls naive enough to fall for your schemes. I orchestrated the deals, attended those godforsaken meetings in dodgy places, and spent hours sewing secret compartments into backpacks and suitcases. What did you do? All you had to do was entertain the stupid idiots and make them think you were going to marry them. It was not exactly hard work on your part!"

The room was so quiet you could hear a pin drop. Lisa's incriminating words hung in the air like a dense fog.

"And for what? All so that you could start your precious investment firm, move to a big house in the suburbs, and buy a motorboat! And now you want to 'come clean'? Now? Haven't you forgotten about Helen? You've spent all our money on that goddamn boat! Every penny goes to that wretched thing. Perhaps you got hit on the head a little too hard and have forgotten that we haven't got any money in the bank—you've bankrupted us with your thoughtless schemes, and *now* you want to come clean!?"

The Thai detectives exchanged glances before locking eyes with Harry. The chief detective gave a small, almost imperceptible nod. Euclid switched off the phone. They had what they needed; Lisa had just incriminated herself in her own words. One of the detectives stopped the recording, ending the high-stakes operation, and made a phone call to the uniformed officers who were waiting at the retreat.

Harry looked at Euclid, her eyes brimming with a blend of relief, triumph, and sadness. "We did it," she finally said.

Lisa sat alone in her hut, her face flushed red with anger. "Can you hear me? Hello? Hello!" she shouted into the phone. But there was only silence; the call had been disconnected.

She was about to redial when the door burst open. Mary and Anthony walked in. "Lisa, please give me my phone," Mary said, her voice firm but tinged with sadness.

"The police are waiting for you outside," Anthony added.

"What police? What are you talking about?" Lisa's confusion was apparent; her mouth was open, but she did not know what to say.

"It's over, Lisa. Everything you've just said has been recorded." Anthony's voice was serious, almost clinical.

"You can't be serious. It's a joke, right?" Her eyes darted between Mary and Anthony.

Before she could get another word out, two police officers stepped into the hut, speaking to her in Thai. Though she didn't understand the language, their body language was unambiguous—they were arresting her.

One of the officers began to recite her rights in Thai as the other clicked his cold steel handcuffs around Lisa's wrists.

Mary's eyes met Lisa's. "It's time for the truth to be told."

Lisa's face paled, a flood of realization dawning on her. Her past had finally caught up with her, and her world was beginning to unravel.

"Wait, wait! You can't believe James. He's a fool!" Lisa was becoming increasingly frantic as the officers led her toward the door, her eyes darting around for any sign of reprieve.

The officers, not understanding English, merely shrugged and continued with their gesticulations that she must go with them.

"What's going on, Mary? What are you people doing to me?" Lisa's voice was tinged with desperation, her eyes wide and fearful.

Mary looked at her, regret and sadness mixed in her gaze. "Lisa, the voice you heard on the phone wasn't James. It was a pre-recorded message. Harry and Euclid used AI to deepfake his voice from a message he had left on Harry's phone before the accident. It turns out Euclid is not only good at mathematics but also quite clever with computers. They've caught everything you've said. You've basically confessed."

"You mean to tell me it was a setup? But why? Why go to all this trouble?" Lisa's face was a cocktail of disbelief, confusion, and rage.

"Because it's time for the truth, Lisa. The truth about you, about James, about all the lives you've wrecked. It's time for justice. Do you remember the girl, Moira? It was Yvonne. Yvonne spent almost a decade in a Thai prison. You destroyed her life; that's why she tried to kill James."

Lisa looked like she had been slapped across the face. As the reality of her situation sank in, her shoulders slumped in defeat. With a final despairing glance at Mary, the officers led her away, her once formidable façade crumbling, revealing her fear of a future of uncertainty and retribution.

"Please check on Clara and tell her that I love her very much," Lisa asked Mary as she left the hut.

Chapter 28

TO THE FUTURE

Golden rays of sunlight streamed through the wooden slats of the restaurant's walls, casting dappled shadows across the well-worn wooden table. The air was rich with the smell of freshly grilled fish, mingled with the salty tang of the sea that wafted through the open windows. Laughter bubbled up from the adjacent tables where local fishermen were enjoying their hard-earned meals, their voices merging with the rhythmic slap of the waves against the dock.

Amaya was the first to break the silence. "So, we're all here safe and sound, and two criminals are behind bars. I still can't believe all of this happened."

Harry corrected her, "Well, two behind bars, one on the loose, and one will be chained to his bed once he wakes up. James is going to have a real shock when he comes out of his coma. The doctors are positive he will recover in the next few days."

Mary looked at Harry with admiration. "What still gets me is your brilliance, Harry. How did you come up with the idea to catch Lisa in such an innovative way?"

Harry shrugged, her eyes twinkling. "Honestly, I got the idea from a true-crime podcast. They were talking about criminals using AI to create deepfake audio to make fraudulent voice messages. In that episode, a man was recounting how he received a distressing phone call from his daughter telling him that she'd been kidnapped. The victim, who was otherwise a very logical and matter-of-fact person, admitted that hearing his daughter's voice made him believe everything that was said. Not once did he doubt the crooks, and he didn't even try to call his daughter, who was supposedly kidnapped, to check if the story was true. He cleared his bank account and transferred his life's savings to the thieves' account. The young woman herself was at work all day, unaware of what her father was going through. It struck me that if technology can be used for ill, it can be flipped to do good too."

Euclid grinned, taking a sip of his iced tea. "Well, I'm just glad I could help in making those recordings. Turning the tables using AI technology was fascinating."

"A little poetic justice, if you ask me," Sarah said, leaning romantically against Euclid.

"I can't say I ever expected our yoga retreat would turn into an episode of a crime show, but I'm glad justice is being served. Do we think the police will be able to find other victims of Lisa and James's enterprise? It's possible some of these women are still in prison. According to the Thai legal system, smuggling narcotics can be punished with a life sentence." Anthony sighed.

Harry tapped her chin thoughtfully. "Given what we've collected, I'd say they have a pretty solid start. And let's not forget that we've stopped them from reinstating their operation in Southeast Asia—there's no doubt in my mind that this is what James was talking about when he was bragging about good investment and money coming in. It was only a matter of time before another vulnerable person would have been recruited to do their dirty work."

"I just hope this makes a difference," Amaya said, looking up. "Do you think Yvonne will come back? I can't believe she left Marieke alone in jail; the woman was willing to kill for her."

"I'm not sure if Yvonne will come back," Harry admitted.

As the sun dipped below the horizon, bathing the room in hues of orange and gold, they raised their glasses, each lost in thought but united in the feeling that, for once, the good guys had come out on top.

"To the future," Harry proposed.

"To the future," they all echoed, clinking their glasses.

Harry looked around the table. "So, what are everyone's plans for the rest of their holidays?"

Sarah snuggled closer to Euclid and grinned. "We've decided to take a trip to the island next door, Koh Phangan."

Mary's eyes lit up. "Oh, that's an excellent idea. There's actually going to be a Full Moon Party soon. It's a once-in-a-lifetime event you shouldn't miss."

Amaya looked puzzled. "A Full Moon Party? What's that?"

Mary leaned back in her chair, her eyes twinkling. "Ah, the Full Moon Party on Koh Phangan. Imagine an entire beach transformed into a sprawling, open-air nightclub. Neon lights everywhere, fire dancers, and crowds of people from every corner of the globe, all there to celebrate the full moon."

Amaya looked intrigued, but it was clear she couldn't quite picture it. Mary continued, her voice tinged with nostalgia, "When I went twenty years ago, it was like a rite of passage. You're in this magical place where the sand is your dance floor, the sky is your ceiling, and the DJ's beats echo the rhythm of the ocean waves. People are painted in fluorescent colors, and the air is a mix of sea salt, sweat, and pure, unfiltered joy."

Sarah's eyes widened, clearly captivated. "Wow, that sounds unreal."

Mary nodded emphatically. "Oh, it's real, and it's incredible. You dance till you can't feel your legs, and just when you think you can't go on, the sun starts to rise. And you find yourself on that same beach, exhausted but euphoric, as the dawn light hits the ocean. It's an experience you'll never forget."

Euclid looked at Sarah. "After hearing all that, I'm not sure if I want to go..."

Sarah laughed. "Don't be a party pooper. Full Moon Party, here we come!"

Euclid's face depicted shock and horror. "Will you go, Harry? Amaya?"

Harry lifted her glass. "Me? If you go, I'll go. I need more material for my blog, so a Full Moon Party might be perfect."

Glasses clinked, sealing the promise of more shared adventures on the horizon.

"It doesn't sound like something I'd enjoy," Amaya admitted. "I'll look for a house-sit somewhere in this area for the rest of my holiday, and then I will travel to Bangkok where I am housesitting two Persian cats for a rich Swiss lady."

Sarah's eyes lit up. "Sounds like fun!"

"I think so," Amaya assured her. "I'll be staying in an old colonial part of the city. I hope to have time to work on my art while I'm there."

Mary stretched out in her chair, interlocking her fingers behind her head. "As for me, I'm in desperate need of a retreat after all this excitement. I might book myself into an ashram in India before heading back to Spain. You all should come to visit if you're ever in Southern Spain."

A wave of agreement swept around the table. "That sounds wonderful, Mary," Harry said, before turning her gaze toward Anthony. "And what about you? What's your plan?"

"I've decided to stay on Koh Samui," Anthony revealed. "I think it's a perfect place for me to retire, and I have some ideas for a small business. Nothing grand or risky. I just want to make enough money to get by."

Sarah raised her glass. "To new beginnings and the friendships we've formed here!"

One by one, everyone lifted their glasses.

Euclid caught the eye of Chariya, the restaurant owner, who had been bustling around, serving dishes and sharing smiles all evening. "Could we get the bill, please?"

The woman shook her head, her eyes twinkling. "No, no bill for you. You saved Lamai, and our whole community is grateful. She is a strong girl, still on a drip in the hospital, but she will be okay. We don't have much crime or many accidents here, so what you did means a lot."

A warm sense of community swept through the group, each touched by the woman's kindness. Harry felt a momentary tug of curiosity. "Chariya, I wanted to ask you about something," Harry said a little hesitantly. "You've lived on this island all your life. Do you remember a boat accident that happened around twenty years ago? Two American tourists died that day."

The woman looked puzzled for a moment before calling out to her husband, who was grilling a large fish on the beach. They exchanged a few words in Thai.

Finally, she turned back to Harry. "I was just checking with my husband if I got the facts right," she explained. "Yes, I think I know which accident you're talking about. A tourist boat was either coming or going to Koh Phangan. It sank not too far from the shore. It was a freak accident. A hurricane came suddenly and overturned the boat before it had a chance to moor. There were many tourists on board, and fortunately most were rescued by the Coast Guard and by local fishermen, but two Americans lost their lives that day. It was very tragic."

Harry locked eyes with the woman. "You see, they were my parents. They were doctors, and they were working for a charity, Doctors Without Borders."

The old woman's eyes widened in confusion. "I'm very sorry to hear that, but are you sure they were working here? We don't have Doctors Without Borders on Koh Samui;

they usually work in the south, near the border, and in more impoverished parts of the country."

"Perhaps they were doing something else here." Harry didn't want to argue with the woman even though she was quite certain that, according to her grandparents' account, her parents had been working when they died. "Is there anyone on the island who might remember more about the accident?"

The owner paused. "There are several people who were also on the boat that day. I could give you names, but they don't speak English. Your best bet might be to speak to the captain."

"The captain?" Harry's eyebrows shot up in surprise.

"Yes," she said, nodding. "The captain went to jail for involuntary manslaughter. He was released after a few years. He lives in a small cottage on Koh Phangan."

Harry glanced at Euclid and Sarah, her eyes meeting theirs. "It must be destiny," she said, her voice tinged with a newfound determination. "If we're heading to Koh Phangan anyway, it seems like I have another reason to go."

It was as if the past had circled back, offering Harry a chance to treat a wound that had never fully healed. And in that small, family-run fishing restaurant, amidst newfound friends and an unfolding adventure, Harry felt ready again to face the events that had left her orphaned.

***

MOONLIT SECRETS

A HARRY SINCLAIR COZY TRAVEL MYSTERY BOOK 2

Get It in Any Major Online Bookshop

Prologue

Sarah woke to the sound of rumbling outboard engines and the smell of salt water mixed with gasoline. Confused and disoriented, she squinted into the dark, trying to make sense of her surroundings. As her eyes adjusted, she realized she was lying on a rough couch inside the cabin of a small motorboat. The cool sea air clung to her skin like a moist veil.

Slowly, she sat up and looked around. Across from her, two Thai women were sitting quietly, tired and absorbed in their own thoughts. They were dressed in party clothes: sequined tops, short skirts, and makeup that was now smudged. Sarah felt a knot tighten in her stomach. What had happened? Where was she? A panicked thought flashed across her mind: *Where are Euclid and Harry?*

She opened her mouth to ask what was going on but then decided to remain silent. Something wasn't right. She looked to the right and saw two older Thai men—one by the boat's engine and another at the boat's wheel. One of the men seemed vaguely familiar, but she couldn't place him; her dull head was pounding too hard for her to think clearly.

Sarah glanced out into the inky darkness of the ocean. Besides the narrow beam of the boat's headlight, the world around her was pitch black. She felt her heart thump loudly against her ribcage as a terrible sense of dread washed over her.

Who are these people? And where are they taking me?

The boat cut swiftly through the water, its destination as murky as the thoughts clouding Sarah's mind. Her instincts screamed that something was profoundly wrong, but her throbbing headache and dizziness made it impossible to think straight.

Chapter 1: On the Ferry

The passengers from Koh Samui to Koh Phangan were an eclectic collection of souls. Thai locals sat alongside sunburnt tourists, who buried their faces in guidebooks or gazed in wonder across the shimmering sea. The scent of algae mixed with wafts of greasy sunblock cream and the occasional spicy aroma of Thai street food that had been carried in small plastic packets onto the boat.

Harry, Euclid, and Sarah found a spot to sit down on, away from the chatty tourists and locals napping on the lower levels of the boat. As they settled into the plastic chairs screwed into the upper deck, the scene ahead was already turning into a picture-postcard view, with the looming shape of Koh Phangan framed by a sky ablaze with pink and orange.

"Thanks for convincing me to come, Sarah. The Full Moon Party is going to make for some great content on my travel blog," Harry said, snapping a few photos with her phone.

Euclid chuckled. "I'm still not entirely sold on the idea, you know. But I do have a few days to decide, right?"

Sarah nudged him playfully. "Exactly! In the meantime, let's just enjoy the beaches. And I know you're itching to go diving."

"Yeah," Euclid said, grinning. "I've heard that Sail Rock and Chumphon Pinnacle are must-visits. Those spots are rich in marine life, and if we're lucky, we might have a chance to see some whale sharks."

"You'll have to go alone on that trip, Euclid," Sarah said, looking serious. "You know I'm not the world's best swimmer, and I feel so nervous on small boats, especially if there are sharks around. I prefer to explore inland."

Harry's eyes lit up. "That sounds amazing! I've read about some stunning waterfalls on the island."

Sarah's eyes widened. "That's an excellent idea. How about we hike through the jungle to see them? Sounds to me like that would be a day well spent."

Sarah leaned back in her chair, her eyes following the raucous seagulls swooping and circling the boat. "So, Harry, what's the name of the resort we're staying at?"

"Mango Moon Hideaway," Harry replied, scrolling through her phone to pull up a picture. "It's a bit secluded, but a high school friend of mine is staying there right now, and she's recommended it."

"That's amazing! Why didn't you mention we were going to meet a friend of yours?"

Harry hesitated, lost for words. "To be honest, Zoë is not a real friend of mine. We grew up in the same town, Ithaca, went to high school together and even worked as reporters in New Your, but somehow, we never clicked. She's just..." Harry's mouth grimaced in discomfort. "It's hard to say what's wrong with her, but you'll meet her, so I don't want to prejudice your opinion. You'll see for yourself. It's hard to explain why Zoë rubs me up the wrong way. Anyway, she's also a travel blogger, and she told me the place is a hidden gem. Apparently, you can just lay in a hammock on your porch and let the sound of the waves lull you to sleep. I've seen photos on her Instagram."

Sarah's eyes closed briefly, picturing the scene. "Oh, that sounds absolutely divine."

Harry hadn't been perfectly honest with her friends when she said that Zoë had recommended Mango Moon Hideaway. Zoë had written to Harry a few days earlier and demanded her help. Her DMs were cryptic, but the plea for assistance was clear.

I know we have not always seen eye to eye, but I've just noticed that you're nearby, and I need help from someone I can trust. I can't explain what it is about, but it's big! This story will set us up for life. See the Google location of the resort where I'm staying below. I hope you can make it. Don't tell anyone that I'm a reporter! See you soon!

Harry was still feeling indignant about the way Zoë had assumed that Harry would rush to her assistance, but then, in all fairness, she could not resist a good story. What was it that Zoë was investigating? She was too close to pass this opportunity. While Harry enjoyed her travel blogging, she had to admit that it was not intellectually challenging. She often struggled to make a fun story out of a sightseeing trip.

Euclid, who had been absorbed with his phone, interrupted Harry's ruminations. "Okay, so I've found the place online. It looks like it's perched right on the cliffs, overlooking the sea. The restaurant and swimming pool are on top, and the huts are spread out, each surrounded by mango and banana trees. It has some pretty solid reviews, mostly from backpackers. Listen to this one: *Epic Foam Parties!*"

Sarah raised an eyebrow, her eyes twinkling with curiosity. "Foam party? What on earth is a foam party?"

Euclid chuckled. "Ah, the classic foam party. The pinnacle of human civilization," he said, his voice tinged with a healthy amount of sarcasm. "Imagine a swimming pool, but it's filled with foam instead of water. People enter said foam-filled pool and dance around like they're auditioning for a laundry detergent commercial. It's truly an unforgettable experience."

Harry burst into laughter. "A laundry detergent commercial? Oh, you're such a poet, Euclid."

"Hey, it's not my cup of tea, but to each their own," he continued, grinning. "Personally, I prefer my pool water without bubbles and my parties without the risk of accidentally getting soap in my eyes."

"Well, I'm with you on that one," Harry said, joining in. "Foam parties might be not be so 'epic' but the resort itself sounds amazing."

"As long as there's an option to not be covered in foam, I think we'll manage," Sarah said, her eyes meeting Harry's.

As the ferry approached Koh Phangan, the three young friends couldn't help but marvel at the island's natural beauty. Verdant hills met the horizon, fringed by shimmering golden beaches that seemed to stretch on forever. Palm trees stood like sentinels along the coastline; beyond them, the dense jungle beckoned with the promise of undiscovered adventures.

Amid the clatter of footsteps and the rustle of bags being gathered by the other passengers, Sarah turned to Harry. "Have you had any luck tracking down the captain of the boat where your parents... you know?"

Harry shook her head, her eyes never leaving the increasingly clear view of the island. "I've got a name, but it's a common one. I'm hoping to ask around when we get there—maybe in some bars or restaurants where the locals hang out."

"Why don't you use Google Translate to search for Thai newspaper articles about the accident?" Euclid chimed in, adjusting his backpack on his shoulders. "It could help, right?"

Harry sighed. "I've tried that. But you know how it is with translations. They don't always make sense. Sometimes, it turns into an incomprehensible mess, and I don't want to make any assumptions based on a bad translation."

Sarah placed her hand reassuringly on Harry's arm. "Well, I hope you find the truth. I can only imagine how much it means to you."

Harry nodded, her eyes now filled with a mix of hope and resolve. "Yeah, me too. Either way, I won't stop looking."

As the ferry docked, the chatter of excited tourists and local commuters filled the air. The three friends grabbed their bags and joined the throng of passengers as they disembarked. Their thoughts were already focused on the adventures awaiting them on Koh Phangan.

The port on the island buzzed with activity as they left the ferry behind. A kaleidoscope of sights and sounds greeted them as they made their way through the lively port. Friendly locals hawked fresh fruits, trinkets, and island maps from makeshift stalls. Travelers—backpackers with dreadlocks, young families with excited kids, and couples holding hands—milled around, their faces flushed with the prospect of the island's many adventures. An array of tuk-tuks, taxis, and scooter rental stands lined the perimeter of the harbor, each manned by keen tour operators who vied for the tourists' attention by means of enthusiastic gestures and calls.

"Wow, this is quite the bustling little harbor," Harry observed, soaking in the atmosphere.

"Yeah, it's got everything from coconuts to sarongs," Euclid agreed. "Speaking of which, we should head to one of those scooter rental places if we want to explore the whole island."

Sarah pointed to a row of shops just beyond the queue of taxis. "Those look promising."

The trio navigated their way through the throngs of people and headed towards the scooter stands. Each rental spot was adorned with various models, all displayed like proud trophies by the stall owners. Rental rates were posted on colorful boards, typically accompanied by pictures of idyllic island destinations to entice potential customers.

"Should we go basic or sporty?" Sarah wondered out loud, eyeing the options.

"Basic is fine by me. We're not entering a Grand Prix," Harry joked.

Euclid laughed. "Agreed. As long as they get us from point A to point B."

After a brief negotiation over the daily rental price and a quick tutorial on how to operate them, they each picked a scooter, strapped on their open-face, retro-style helmets, and set off. As they left the port behind, Harry couldn't help but feel that this was the beginning of something unforgettable. With the wind in their hair and the smell of the ocean filling their senses, they rode steadily towards Mango Moon Hideaway, Euclid leading the way, his phone securely mounted on his handlebar for easy navigation.

They soon turned off the main road, leaving the bustling port area behind, and followed entered a track shrouded by lush jungle. A dappled canopy of leaves overhead filtered the sunlight, casting playful shadows across the dirt trail. Their scooters hummed along in harmony with the songs of cicadas and exotic birds, which seemed to guide them deeper into the island's tropical heart.

"Wow, this is stunning!" Sarah called out from behind Harry, her eyes wide with wonder. "Look at all the colors!"

Indeed, the track was flanked by an explosion of flora—wild orchids with their vibrant hues, ruby-red hibiscus flowers, and flamboyant plumeria in whites and pinks. They rode past groves of coconut palms and towering rubber trees, their leaves shimmering in the occasional shafts of piercing sunlight that broke through the canopy.

As they climbed a steep hill, the forest began to thin, offering flashing glimpses of the cerulean sea below. Harry's heart swelled as they reached the top, where a viewpoint clearing revealed a breathtaking panorama: a sparkling blue-green bay on one side and, in the distance, the misty majestic silhouettes of Koh Tao and Koh Nang Yuan. The sight was so beautiful and tranquil that Harry momentarily forgot the dark question that had brought her to Thailand.

After soaking in the view and taking some photos, they descended the other side of the hill, following the winding trail indicated on Euclid's phone. Before long, a rustic wooden sign came into view, with the words 'Mango Moon Hideaway' hand-painted in bright colors.

As they rode through the entrance to the resort compound, it was clear they had arrived at a slice of paradise. Nestled among the jungle foliage, the resort was a secluded haven. The restaurant and pool area was perched atop a small cliff with a panoramic view of the sea and surrounding islands. Wooden huts, each adorned with a small porch and a hammock, were tucked away below the cliff, almost hidden by a curtain of tropical greenery.

"Wow," Sarah said, breathing heavily as they dismounted their scooters. "This place is divine."

Harry grinned, taking off her helmet. "I told you it was worth the ride."

Walking toward the reception area, they passed clusters of young people, their skin slightly pink from the sun and saltwater, towels draped over shoulders or tied around waists. A couple of young lovers held each other by the elbow as they shook the sand out of their flip-flops, while others chatted and laughed under the trees, recounting tales of their underwater adventures.

"Hey, how's it going?" one guy greeted them, waving cheerfully, a surfboard tucked under his arm. "Welcome to paradise!"

CONTINUE READING *MOONLIT SECRETS*

To receive the news of the latest releases in the Harry Sinclair Cozy Travel Mystery series, sign up with your email via her website.

www.sabinaostrowska.com

Sign up here!

Or simply follow her on social media:

Facebook @sabinawriter

Instagram @sabina.author or @harrysinclair.cozymystery

TikTok @sabina.author

So far in Harry Sinclair series:

Check out Sabina's bestselling non-fiction humorous series about starting a new life in Andalusia:

Harry Sinclair Koh Samui Recipes

DISCOVERING SUSHI IN THAILAND

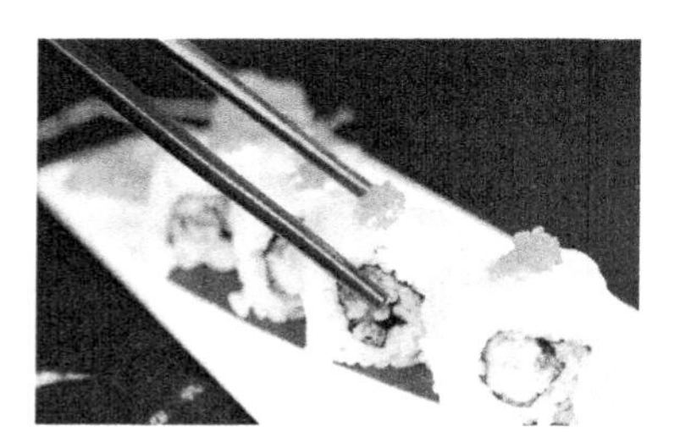

Hello, fellow travelers and food enthusiasts! It's Harry here, coming to you with another slice of my culinary journey. Today, I want to talk about a surprising discovery I made in Thailand – their love for sushi!

Yes, you read that right. While Thailand is world-renowned for its mouthwatering local cuisine, I was amazed to find out how much the Thai people adore sushi. But before we dive into the delightful world of sushi as it is experienced in Thailand, let me share with you some of my newfound appreciation for this exquisite Japanese cuisine, especially when paired with a crisp glass of Chardonnay.

My favorite dish, California Rolls, are also very popular in Thailand, but with a twist. Instead of using traditional avocado, crabmeat, and cucumber, Thai sushi chefs love to add mango and papaya into the mix. These ingredients not only add a burst of color but also an unexpected sweetness that tantalizes the palate.

Ingredients:

Sushi rice (1 cup, cooked and seasoned with sushi vinegar)

Nori sheets

Fresh mango, thinly sliced

Cooked shrimp, halved

Cucumber, julienned

Avocado, thinly sliced

Soy sauce, wasabi, and sweet chili sauce for dipping

Instructions:

1. Lay out your bamboo sushi mat and place a sheet of nori on it.

2. Spread a thin layer of sushi rice over the nori, leaving about an inch free at the top.

3. In the middle of the rice, lay down your strips of mango, shrimp, cucumber, and avocado.

4. Carefully roll the sushi using the bamboo mat, pressing gently but firmly to ensure the roll is tight.

5. With a sharp, wet knife, slice the roll into bite-sized pieces.

6. Serve with soy sauce, a dab of wasabi, and a side of sweet chili sauce for that Thai-inspired kick!

Now, what's sushi without a little wine to elevate the experience? While I'm a fan of pairing sushi with Chardonnay, the sweet and spicy flavors of this particular roll might be complemented better by a Riesling or a Pinot Gris. These wines, with their fruity notes and crisp acidity, can hold their own against the rich flavors of the sushi and the spicy kick of the chili sauce.

So, there you have it, folks – a little slice of my Thai adventure wrapped up in a sushi roll. Whether you're a sushi aficionado or a curious foodie, I encourage you to give this recipe a try. It's a delightful way to bring a taste of Thailand into your kitchen and pair it with your favorite wine for a truly exquisite culinary experience.

Until next time, keep exploring, keep tasting, and as always, keep sharing those incredible food stories. Cheers!

MANGO STICKY RICE

Hello, beautiful adventurers! It's Harry Sinclair here, your globetrotting companion, back with another delicious discovery from my travels. This time, I'm bringing you a mouthful of tropical paradise from the sundrenched shores of Koh Samui, Thailand. Picture this: crystal-clear waters, balmy evenings, and the sweet, comforting taste of Mango Sticky Rice. It's not just a dish; it's an amazing experience—one that I was lucky enough to have in a quaint little restaurant nestled in the heart of this island paradise.

Mango Sticky Rice is a classic Thai dessert known locally as Khao Niew Mamuang. It's a simple yet utterly divine combination of glutinous rice, creamy coconut milk, ripe mangoes, and a sprinkle of crispy mung beans or sesame seeds. After having my taste buds enchanted in Koh Samui, I knew I had to bring this recipe back for you all to try. And don't worry if you're thinking, "But Harry, where on earth will I find Thai ingredients?" I've got you covered with some handy substitutions to make this dish, no matter where you are in the US.

Ingredients:

1 cup glutinous (sticky) rice: Available in the Asian section of most supermarkets or online. If you can't find it, sushi rice can be a good substitute, though the texture will be slightly different.

1 1/4 cups water

1 can (13.5 oz) coconut milk: Make sure to use full-fat coconut milk for that creamy goodness.

1/2 cup sugar: Adjust according to your sweet tooth.

1/2 teaspoon salt

2 ripe mangoes: Look for ones that are sweet and soft to the touch. If mangoes are out of season, canned mango pulp is a decent backup.

Optional toppings: Toasted mung beans or sesame seeds. If these are hard to come by, try crushed peanuts for a crunchy finish.

Let's Get Cooking:

1. Rinse and Soak the Rice: Begin by washing the sticky rice under cold water until the water runs clear. Then, soak it in water for at least an hour or overnight if you're a plan-ahead kind of person. This step is crucial for achieving that perfect, sticky texture.

2. Steam the Rice: Drain the rice and steam it. If you don't have a steamer, you can improvise with a sieve or colander over a pot of boiling water. Cover and let it steam for about 15-20 minutes, or until tender and translucent.

3. Coconut Milk Magic: While the rice is steaming, grab a saucepan and mix the coconut milk, sugar, and salt over medium heat until dissolved. Don't let it boil—we're not trying to make coconut soup here!

4. Marry the Rice and Coconut Milk: Once the rice is done, transfer it to a bowl and pour about 3/4 of the coconut milk mixture over it. Stir gently and let it sit for about 30 minutes to soak up all that coconutty goodness.

5. Slice the Mangoes: Peel the mangoes and cut the flesh into thick slices. If you're using canned mango, drain the syrup and pat the slices dry.

6. Assemble and Serve: Scoop a generous serving of the sticky rice onto a plate, arrange the mango slices around it, and drizzle the remaining coconut milk over the top. Sprinkle with your chosen topping for that extra crunch.

7. Enjoy!: Dig in and let each bite transport you to the serene beaches of Koh Samui. You can almost hear the waves, can't you?

There you have it, my fellow wanderlusters—a taste of Thailand from the comfort of your home. Mango Sticky Rice is more than just a dessert; it's a reminder of the beauty and simplicity of the world's best cuisines. It's my hope that this recipe not only satisfies your sweet tooth but also ignites a spark of curiosity to explore new cultures and flavors.

Until our next adventure, stay hungry for life and all its delicious moments!

GRILLED SEA BASS WITH A THAI TWIST

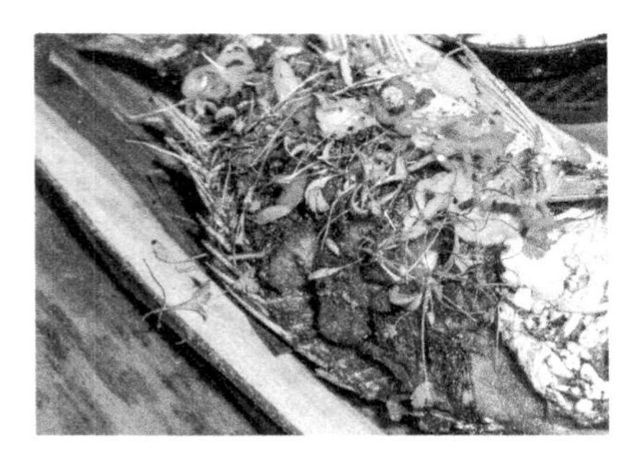

Ahoy, my culinary explorers and seafaring friends! It's Harry Sinclair here, your guide to the globe's most tantalizing tastes. Today, I'm thrilled to share with you a recipe that will sail straight into your heart: a Grilled Sea Bass (or Snapper) stuffed with Lemongrass and Lime Leaves, inspired by a magical day spent navigating the emerald waters of Mu Ko Ang Thong National Park in Thailand.

Imagine this: you're aboard a traditional Thai boat, the sea breeze wafting through your hair, the sun kissing your skin, and then, you're served the most divine fish dish that's so full of flavor. It's like Thailand is serenading your taste buds. I knew I had to bring this culinary delight to you with a few tweaks to make it easy for you to recreate it in your American kitchen.

Ingredients:

1 whole sea bass or snapper (about 2 to 3 pounds, cleaned and scaled): If you can't find sea bass or snapper, any firm white fish will do the trick.

2 stalks of lemongrass: Finely chopped. If lemongrass is hard to come by, a zest of lemon can add a similar citrusy fragrance.

A handful of lime leaves: Sliced thinly. Substitute with lime zest if lime leaves are not available.

2 cloves of garlic: Minced because garlic makes everything taste better.

2 tablespoons of fish sauce: This is the secret to that umami-rich Thai flavor. Soy sauce can work as a substitute if necessary.

1 tablespoon of soy sauce: For a bit of depth to the marinade.

1 teaspoon of sugar: Just a touch to balance the flavors.

Juice of 1 lime: For that zesty kick.

Salt and pepper to taste.

Garnish: A few sprigs of cilantro and lime wedges to serve.

Let's Get Grilling:

1. Prep the Fish: Start by making shallow diagonal cuts on both sides of the fish. This not only looks pretty but also helps the flavors penetrate the flesh and speeds up the cooking time.

2. Flavor Bomb: In a bowl, mix the finely chopped lemongrass (or lemon zest), sliced lime leaves (or lime zest), minced garlic, fish sauce, soy sauce, sugar, and lime juice. Whisk it together until the sugar dissolves.

3. Stuff and Marinate: Rub the mixture generously inside and outside the fish, making sure some of it gets into the cuts you made earlier. Stuff the cavity with any leftover lemongrass and lime leaves. Let it marinate for at least 30 minutes, or even better, overnight in the fridge if you're planning ahead.

4. Grill to Perfection: Preheat your grill to medium-high heat. Grill the fish for about 7-10 minutes on each side or until the skin is crisp and the flesh flakes easily with a fork. The exact time will depend on the size of your fish, so keep an eye on it.

5. Serve with Love: Transfer your beautifully grilled fish onto a platter. Garnish with fresh cilantro and lime wedges on the side. Squeeze a bit of lime over it right before you dig in, and voilà, you've got yourself a Thai-inspired feast!

There's something special about cooking and eating fish that's been kissed by flames and imbued with the essence of lemongrass and lime leaves—it's like each bite is ready to transport you to a far-off land. This dish isn't just a recipe; it's a journey, a memory of azure seas, and the taste of adventure.

So, my dear readers, whether you're longing for the taste of Thailand or simply looking for a delicious way to spice up your dinner routine, this Grilled Sea Bass with Lemongrass and Lime Leaves is your ticket to a culinary adventure. Here's to making every meal an exploration and every bite a discovery.

Bon appétit, or as they say in Thailand, *gin hai aroy*!

THE THAI-INSPIRED MAI TAI

Hey there, my fellow cocktail connoisseurs and travel enthusiasts! It's your favorite wanderer, Harry Sinclair, back again with some liquid sunshine from my recent escapades in the vibrant country of Thailand. If there's one thing that rivals the beauty of Thailand's beaches, it's the country's rich and tantalizing cocktail scene. Today, I'm thrilled to share with you recipes for two cocktails that capture the essence of Thai flavors and hospitality: the Mai Tai and the Thai Basil Mojito. So, grab your shaker, and let's transport your taste buds to the Land of Smiles with these easy-to-make, refreshing concoctions.

The Mai Tai is a classic cocktail that's synonymous with tropical relaxation. While not originally from Thailand, this version adds a Thai twist that makes it utterly irresistible.

Ingredients:

2 oz white rum: Choose a good quality rum for the best flavor.

1 oz dark rum: For that rich, deep flavor.

1/2 oz lime juice: Freshly squeezed, please!

1/2 oz orange curaçao: This adds a lovely citrusy sweetness.

1/4 oz simple syrup: Easy to make at home by dissolving equal parts sugar and water.

1/4 oz orgeat syrup: This almond-flavored syrup is key to an authentic Mai Tai.

Crushed ice

Garnish: A lime wedge and a sprig of mint or a slice of pineapple for that tropical look.

Let's Mix:

1. Combine and Shake: In a shaker, combine the white rum, lime juice, orange curaçao, simple syrup, and orgeat syrup with a handful of crushed ice. Shake well until the mixture is chilled.

2. Strain and Top: Strain the mixture into a glass filled with crushed ice, then gently pour the dark rum over the top to create a layered effect.

3. Garnish and Serve: Garnish with your lime wedge, mint, or pineapple slice. Take a sip, close your eyes, and let the flavors take you straight to a beachside bar in Phuket.

THAI BASIL MOJITO

This twist on the classic Mojito incorporates Thai basil, adding a unique anise-like flavor that pairs wonderfully with the freshness of mint and lime.

Ingredients:

10 fresh mint leaves: For that refreshing mojito signature.

5 Thai basil leaves: If you can't find Thai basil, regular basil can work in a pinch, thoughthe flavor will be slightly different.

2 oz white rum

1 oz lime juice

2 tablespoons sugar: Adjust to taste.

Soda water: To top off your drink and add fizz.

Garnish: A sprig of Thai basil or mint and a lime wheel.

Let's Mix:

1. Muddle It Up:In a sturdy glass, muddle the mint leaves, Thai basil, sugar, and lime juice together. You're aiming to just bruise the leaves to release their oils, not shred them to bits.

2. Add Rum: Pour the white rum into the glass and mix well to dissolve the sugar.

3. Ice, Ice, Baby:Fill the glass with ice, then top off with soda water. Stir gently to combine.

4. Garnish and Serve: Add a sprig of Thai basil or mint and a lime wheel for garnish. Each sip is like a refreshing breeze from the Gulf of Thailand.

And there you have it, my dear readers—two Thai-inspired cocktails that are sure to be a hit at your next gathering or when you're simply dreaming of your next adventure .Whether you're a seasoned mixologist or a curious newbie, these recipes are a foolproof way to add some exotic flair to your home bar repertoire.

Remember, the essence of Thai cuisine and cocktails is all about balance—sweet, sour, salty,and bitter, all in perfect harmony. So, don't be afraid to tweak the recipes to suit your taste. After all, the best part of traveling (and mixology!) is putting your own spin on the experiences you gather along the way.

Until our next journey, keep mixing, sipping, and dreaming!

HARRY'S GO-TO EGG OMELET

Good morning, radiant souls! It's Harry Sinclair here, your ambassador of all things delicious and adventurous. If there's one thing I've learned from my sun-soaked days in Koh Samui, it's that a vibrant morning meal sets the tone for a day full of exploration and wonder. Today, I'm beyond excited to share with you my morning secrets from the Land of Smiles: a simple yet utterly satisfying Egg Omelet and a couple of Koh Samui-inspired Breakfast Smoothies that will have you starting your day on a high note, no matter where in the world you wake up.

This omelet isn't just a dish; it's a canvas, ready to be painted with the flavors of Thailand or your own favorite ingredients. It's light, fluffy, and filled with the fresh, vibrant tastes of the local markets.

Ingredients:

2-3 large eggs: For that rich, fluffy base.

1 tablespoon of milk: This is my little secret for an extra fluffy texture. Coconut milk is a fantastic option for a Thai twist.

Salt and pepper to taste

1 tablespoon of olive oil or butter: For cooking.

Fillings: Here's where you can get creative. I love using a combination of diced tomatoes, sliced green onions, and a sprinkle of cheese. For a Thai-inspired touch, add some chopped Thai basil or coriander.

Let's Make It:

1. Whisk It Up: Beat the eggs, milk, salt, and pepper together until well combined.

2. Heat It: Warm the oil or butter in a small nonstick skillet over medium heat.

3. Cook to Perfection: Pour in the egg mixture. As it cooks, add your fillings.

4. Fold and Serve: When the egg mixture is almost set, gently fold the omelet in half over the fillings, let it sit for a moment to cook through, flip it onto the other side for a minute or so, and then slide it onto a plate. Voilà, breakfast is served!

TROPICAL BREAKFAST SMOOTHIES

Nothing says "good morning" like a refreshing smoothie, bursting with the flavors of tropical fruits. Here are two of my favorites that bring a taste of Koh Samui into your home.

Tropical Sunshine Smoothie

1 cup of pineapple chunks: Fresh or frozen for that sweet, tangy kick.

1 ripe mango, peeled and cubed: For a smooth, creamy texture.

1/2 banana: To add sweetness and body.

1/2 cup of coconut milk: For that silky, tropical flavor.

A handful of ice cubes: For a cool, refreshing start.

Koh Samui Banana Smoothie

2 ripe bananas: The star of the show, offering sweetness and creaminess.

1/2 cup of Greek yogurt: For a protein boost and a smooth texture.

1/4 cup of coconut milk: To bring a touch of the tropics.

A drizzle of honey or a sprinkle of cinnamon (optional) for added sweetness or warmth.

A handful of ice: For that chilled, frothy finish.

Blend all ingredients until smooth. Pour into a glass and enjoy a sip of tropical paradise.

My mornings in Koh Samui were filled with the simple joy of these recipes, each bite and sip infused with the island's natural bounty and serene beauty. Now, no matter where I am, whipping up these breakfast delights transports me back to those blissful, sunlit shores.

I hope these recipes bring a taste of Koh Samui's serene mornings to your table. Here's to starting every day with a burst of flavor and a heart full of adventure!

GRILLED TIGER PRAWNS

Hello, fellow wanderlusters! It's Harry here, your go-to gal for all things travel and taste. Today, I'm taking you to a little slice of heaven I discovered in the heart of Fisherman Village in Koh Samui. This quaint, picturesque spot isn't just about stunning sunsets and the gentle lapping of waves; it's a paradise for seafood aficionados like myself. And let me tell you, I've found my new obsession: grilled tiger prawns and an authentic Thai fish curry that will make your taste buds dance the tango!

I couldn't leave this island without uncovering the secrets to these delicious dishes, and so I asked the chef of a quaint little restaurant to share his recipes with me, which he kindly agreed to. And because I believe in spreading joy and deliciousness, I'm passing these culinary treasures on to you!

Grilled Tiger Prawns

Ingredients:

8 large tiger prawns, shell on

2 tablespoons olive oil

1 tablespoon minced garlic

1 tablespoon of fresh ginger

1 teaspoon chili flakes (adjust to taste)

1 tablespoon soy sauce

Juice of 1 lime

Freshly ground black pepper

A handful of fresh coriander for garnish

Instructions:

1. Prep the Prawns: Rinse the tiger prawns and pat them dry. With a sharp knife, make a shallow cut along each prawn's back and remove the vein.

2. Marinate: In a bowl, whisk together olive oil, minced garlic, ginger, chili flakes, soy sauce, lime juice, and a dash of black pepper. Coat the prawns in this marinade and let them sit for about 15-30 minutes.

3. Grill to Perfection: Heat your grill to medium-high. Place the prawns on the grill and cook for about 2-3 minutes on each side or until they turn pink and slightly charred.

4. Serve with Style: Garnish with fresh coriander and a squeeze of lime juice. Perfect for a beachy barbecue or a cozy dinner under the stars.

THAI FISH CURRY

Ingredients:

500g firm white fish fillets (e.g., cod or tilapia), cut into chunks

2 tablespoons vegetable oil

1 onion, finely chopped

2 garlic cloves, minced

1 tablespoon Thai red curry paste

400ml coconut milk

1 tablespoon fish sauce

1 teaspoon palm sugar (or brown sugar)

1 red bell pepper, sliced

A handful of Thai basil leaves

Juice of 1 lime

Instructions:

1. Sauté: Heat oil in a large pan over medium heat. Add onion and garlic, sautéing until soft. Stir in the curry paste and cook for a minute until aromatic.

2. Simmer the Curry: Pour in the coconut milk, fish sauce, and palm sugar, bringing to a gentle simmer. Add the fish and bell pepper, cooking until the fish is just cooked through.

3. Finishing Touches: Remove from heat and stir in the Thai basil and lime juice. Adjust seasoning to taste.

4. Serve and Enjoy: Serve hot with steamed jasmine rice, ready to transport you back to the shores of Koh Samui.

These dishes are more than just meals; they're a journey through the flavors and traditions of Thailand. Grilling the prawns under the open sky or simmering a pot of fish curry brings Koh Samui into your kitchen, no matter where you are in the world.

As I bid farewell to Fisherman Village, with its warm, friendly people and unforgettable flavors, I'm reminded of why I travel: to connect, to discover, and to savor every moment.

Until next time, keep exploring, keep tasting, and, as always, keep sharing the joy!

WINE PAIRINGS FOR THAI CUISINE PLUS BASIL CHILI SQUID RECIPE

Hello, my fellow Epicureans! It's Harry again, your globetrotting companion in all things delicious. Today, I'm embarking on a vinous adventure through the vibrant world of Thai cuisine. Thai food, with its symphony of sweet, sour, spicy, and salty flavors, might seem challenging to pair with wine. But fear not! I've uncorked the secrets to the perfect wine pairings for these exotic dishes, ensuring your next Thai meal is an absolute palate-pleaser.

And because no culinary exploration is complete without a little cooking, I'll also share my latest obsession: a basil chili squid recipe that's as easy to make as it is impressive. Trust me; it's a game-changer.

The Art of Pairing Wine with Thai Food

Thai cuisine is known for its complexity and balance, making the wine pairing an exciting challenge. Here are a few guidelines to enhance your dining experience:

Riesling: The aromatic profile and acidity of a Riesling, especially those with a hint of sweetness, make it a versatile companion for Thai dishes, balancing the heat and complementing the flavors.

Gewürztraminer: This wine, with its notes of lychee, rose petal, and spice, mirrors the aromatic spices in Thai food, making it an excellent match for curry-based dishes or spicy salads.

Rosé: A dry Rosé, with its crisp acidity and berry flavors, is refreshing against the heat of Thai dishes, making it perfect for pairing with seafood and noodle dishes.

Pinot Noir: For those who prefer red wine, a light-bodied Pinot Noir can complement Thai dishes without overwhelming them, especially with recipes featuring tamarind or peanut sauces.

Basil Chili Squid

Now, let's dive into the kitchen with a Thai-inspired recipe that's sure to impress: Basil Chili Squid. This dish is a beautiful showcase of Thai flavors, and it pairs wonderfully with a glass of chilled Riesling or a crisp Rosé, depending on your preference.

Ingredients:

500g fresh squid, cleaned and cut into rings

2 tablespoons vegetable oil

4 garlic cloves, minced

2 fresh red chilies, finely sliced (adjust to taste)

1 red bell pepper, julienned

1 cup Thai basil leaves

2 tablespoons fish sauce

1 tablespoon soy sauce

1 teaspoon sugar

Juice of 1 lime

Freshly ground black pepper

Instructions:

1. Prep the Squid: Make sure the squid is thoroughly cleaned, dried, and cut into bite-sized rings.

2. Sauté: Heat oil in a large skillet or wok over a high heat. Add garlic and chilies, stir-frying until fragrant. Quickly add the squid and bell pepper, stir-frying for 2-3 minutes until the squid is just cooked through and opaque.

3. Flavor Bomb: Lower the heat to medium. Add the fish sauce, soy sauce, and sugar, tossing well to coat the squid evenly. Cook for another minute.

4. Finishing Touches: Remove from heat, and immediately stir in the Thai basil leaves and lime juice. Season with freshly ground black pepper to taste.

5. Serve and Enjoy: Dish out this aromatic delight with steamed jasmine rice or enjoy it as a standalone appetizer. Pair with your chosen wine for an unforgettable dining experience.

So, here's to adventures in taste and to exploring the world one dish (and one glass) at a time. Until our next culinary journey, keep savoring the flavors and the moments.

Cheers, and happy cooking!

For more recipes, follow me on Instagram @harrysinclair.cozymystery

PINEAPPLE FRIED RICE SERVED IN A PINEAPPLE SHELL

Aloha, culinary adventurers! It's your favorite flavor chaser, Harry, back with another exotic getaway that you can recreate right in your kitchen. Today, I'm whisking you away to the sandy shores and swaying palms with a dish that's as visually stunning as it is delectably satisfying: Pineapple Fried Rice served in a pineapple shell. This dish isn't just a meal; it's a voyage to the tropics with every bi te!

But what's a journey without a little customization? Fear not, my fellow home chefs, especially those navigating the aisles of American supermarkets, I've got you covered with easy swaps for those hard-to-find Thai ingredients, ensuring your culinary expedition is smooth sailing.

This dish combines the sweetness of pineapple with the savory flavors of fried rice, creating a perfect balance. Served in a carved-out pineapple shell, it's a feast for the eyes as well as the palate.

Ingredients:

1 large pineapple

2 cups cooked jasmine rice, cooled (preferably left overnight)

2 tablespoons vegetable oil

2 cloves garlic, minced

1 small onion, diced

1/2 cup mixed vegetables (carrots, peas, and corn)

1/2 cup cooked shrimp (optional)

1/2 cup diced ham or chicken (optional)

2 eggs, lightly beaten

2 tablespoons soy sauce

1 tablespoon curry powder (for a Thai twist)

Salt and pepper to taste

A handful of roasted cashews

Fresh cilantro and sliced green onions for garnish

Instructions:

1. Prepare the Pineapple: Cut the pineapple in half, lengthwise. Hollow out each half to create two "bowls," leaving a border. Dice the pineapple flesh for the fried rice.

2. Sauté: Heat oil in a large pan or wok. Add garlic and onion, cooking until fragrant. Stir in the mixed vegetables, cooked shrimp, and ham or chicken, if you are using these meats.

3. The Rice: Add the cooled rice, breaking up any clumps. Stir fry until everything is well combined and the rice starts to get crispy.

4. Flavor Time: Push the rice mixture to the side of the pan. Add the beaten eggs to the other side and scramble. Mix everything together. Stir in the diced pineapple, soy sauce, and curry powder. Season with salt and pepper.

5. Presentation: Spoon the fried rice into the pineapple shells. Garnish with cashews, cilantro, and green onions.

Variations and Substitutions

Rice: No jasmine rice? Basmati or even long-grain rice can be a good substitute. The key is to use rice that's been cooled, as it fries up better than fresh, warm rice.

Protein: Can't find traditional Thai proteins? Any cooked protein will do. For a vegetarian twist, think outside the box with tofu, tempeh, or even edamame.

Soy Sauce Swap: If soy sauce is too strong, try using tamari or a light fish sauce for that umami flavor without the saltiness.

Curry Powder: While not traditionally Thai, curry powder adds an exotic touch that mimics some Thai spices. If you have access to Thai curry paste, it's a fantastic way to add authentic flavor.

Vegetables: Use any vegetables you have on hand. Bell peppers, zucchini, and broccoli all make excellent additions. The goal is to add color and crunch.

This pineapple fried rice is more than just a dish; it's a journey. With each bite, you're transported to a world where the flavors are as vibrant and lively as the Thai landscapes. And with these variations and substitutions, you can bring a slice of the tropics into your home, no matter where you are in the USA.

So, don your chef's hat, and let's turn dinner time into a tropical getaway. Until our next culinary adventure, keep exploring, tasting, and enjoying the world one dish at a time!

COCONUT DREAMS

Hello, lovely wanderers and cocktail aficionados! Harry Sinclair here, your globetrotting guide to all things delicious and intoxicating. Today, I'm bringing the spirit of Koh Samui to your home bar with some dreamy coconut rum-based cocktails that captured my heart (and taste buds) during my island adventures. Whether it was watching the sunset over Lamai Beach or finding serenity in the Secret Buddha Garden, these cocktails were my faithful companions, adding an extra layer of tropical bliss to each moment.

Coconut rum embodies the essence of Koh Samui, with its sweet, creamy flavor that instantly transports you to a world of white sandy beaches and swaying palms. I'm excited to share these recipes with you, along with some handy substitutions for our friends who might be whipping these up in the States. Let's dive into these coconut-infused creations that are sure to make your spirit soar and your heart long for the ocean's call.

Koh Samui Coconut Sunset

This cocktail is a vibrant homage to the breathtaking sunsets of Koh Samui, blending the flavors of coconut, pineapple, and citrus to create a tropical masterpiece.

Ingredients:

2 oz coconut rum: For that smooth, coconutty base. If coconut rum isn't available, feel free to use regular white rum and a splash of coconut water or coconut cream.

2 oz pineapple juice: For a sweet, tropical tang.

1 oz orange juice: Adds a lovely citrus note.

Splash of grenadine: For that gorgeous sunset gradient.

Ice cubes

Garnish: A slice of pineapple or an orange wheel to garnish.

Let's Mix:

1. Shake It Up: In a shaker, combine the coconut rum, pineapple juice, and orange juice with ice. Shake well until chilled.

2. Create the Sunset: Strain the mixture into a glass filled with ice, and slowly pour the grenadine over the top. Watch as it creates a beautiful sunset effect in your glass.

3. Garnish and Enjoy: Add your pineapple slice or orange wheel to garnish. Cheers to a Koh Samui evening, wherever you are!

SAMUI COCONUT BREEZE

This cocktail is as refreshing as a gentle breeze on Chaweng Beach, combining coconut rum with cucumber and lime for a crisp, revitalizing sip.

Ingredients:

2 oz coconut rum

1 oz lime juice: Freshly squeezed for that zesty kick.

2 oz soda water: For a bit of fizz.

Cucumber slices: A few thin slices to infuse the drink with a fresh, clean taste.

Mint leaves: For that aromatic freshness.

Ice cubes

Garnish: A sprig of mint or a lime wheel.

Let's Mix:

1. Muddle It: In a glass, muddle a few cucumber slices and mint leaves to release their flavors.

2. Combine: Add the coconut rum and lime juice, and fill the glass with ice.

3. Top It Off: Pour soda water over the mixture to fill the glass.

4. Garnish and Sip: Add a sprig of mint or a lime wheel for that extra touch. Sip and let the flavors transport you to the serene coasts of Koh Samui.

Embracing the spirit of Koh Samui in your home is about more than just the flavors; it's about capturing the essence of island life—relaxed, joyful, and immersed in natural beauty. These coconut rum-based cocktails are my gift to you, a way to bring a tiny piece of my journey into your world.

So, my dear friends, as you mix these drinks, imagine the soft sands between your toes, the gentle sea breeze, and the warm, welcoming smiles of Koh Samui's inhabitants. Here's to adventures in our hearts and cocktails in our hands!

PAD KRA PAO OR THAI BASIL CHICKEN

Greetings, culinary adventurers and lovers of all things flavorful! Harry Sinclair here, whisking you away on another gastronomic journey to the vibrant streets of Thailand. Today, I'm excited to share with you a dish that holds a special place in the heart of Thai culture and cuisine: Thai Basil Chicken. Known for its bold flavors and simple preparation, this beloved stir-fry dish is a testament to the beauty of Thai cooking, offering a harmonious blend of spicy, sweet, and savory in every bite.

Pad Kra Pao is a staple in Thai households and the street food scene alike, celebrated for its hearty warmth and comforting simplicity. Its name, translating to "stir-fried with basil," reveals the essence of this dish, which is as soul-satisfying as it is delicious. Here, I'll guide you through creating your own Pad Kra Pao, complete with substitutions for our American kitchens and a vegetarian twist for those seeking a plant-based delight.

Ingredients:

1 lb ground chicken: Turkey or pork can also be used as substitutes.

2 tablespoons of cooking oil: Vegetable or canola oil works best for stir-frying.

3-4 cloves of garlic, finely minced: Essential for that aromatic base.

2-3 Thai chilies, finely sliced: Adjust according to your heat preference. Jalapeños or serrano peppers can be used as substitutes if Thai chilies are not available.

1 bell pepper, sliced: Not traditional, but adds a nice crunch and sweetness.

2 tablespoons soy sauce: This will add the savory depth. Light soy sauce is preferred for a more authentic taste.

1 tablespoon oyster sauce: For a rich, umami flavor. Vegetarians can opt for a mushroom sauce or vegan oyster sauce.

1 tablespoon fish sauce: A cornerstone of Thai cuisine, adding a salty depth. Soy sauce mixed with a little bit of seaweed can mimic the umami for a vegetarian version.

1 teaspoon sugar: To balance the flavors.

A generous handful of Thai basil leaves: If you can't find Thai basil, regular basil can work in a pinch, though the flavor will be slightly different.

Serve with steamed jasmine rice.

Let's Cook:

1. Heat It Up: Heat the oil in a large skillet or wok over medium-high heat. Add the garlic and chilies, stir-frying until aromatic.

2. Add the Chicken: Increase the heat to high, add the ground chicken, breaking it apart and stir-frying until it's nearly cooked through.

3. Sauce It: Add the bell pepper, then stir in the soy sauce, oyster sauce, fish sauce, and sugar. Mix well and cook until the chicken is fully cooked.

4. Basil Time: Turn off the heat and stir in the Thai basil leaves until wilted.

5. Serve: Spoon your delicious Pad Kra Pao over a warm bed of jasmine rice and enjoy!

Vegetarian Pad Kra Pao

Swapping the chicken for firm tofu or a mix of mushrooms (like shiitake and button mushrooms) can create a delightful, meat-free version of this dish. Follow the same steps, ensuring to press your tofu beforehand to remove excess water for a better texture when stir-frying.

Pad Kra Pao's importance in Thai culture cannot be overstated. It's a dish that reflects the Thai philosophy of balance, blending the heat from the chilies, the umami from the sauces, the sweetness from the sugar, and the unique aroma of Thai basil. It's a culinary expression of harmony and mindfulness, qualities deeply revered in Thai culture.

Whether you're cooking up the classic chicken version or the vegetarian alternative, making Pad Kra Pao at home is a beautiful way to bring the spirit of Thailand into your kitchen. It's a reminder of the joy found in simple, nourishing meals and the universal language of delicious food.

So, my fellow flavor seekers, as you savor your steaming bowl of Pad Kra Pao, remember that every dish has a story, every ingredient a journey. Here's to adding your own chapter to the rich tapestry of world cuisine.

Happy cooking and joyful eating!

For more recipes, follow me on Instagram @harrysinclair.cozymystery

About the Author

Sabina Ostrowska also known to cozy mystery readers as Sabina O. is the author behind the bestselling 'New Life in Andalusia' series. Enjoying life among the sunny olive groves of southern Spain, Sabina crafts her narratives with a vivid sense of place. 'Shadows of Serenity,' her latest work, marks the debut of her cozy travel mystery series. Here, she invites readers on armchair adventures that span the globe. So pour a glass of your favorite wine and delve into these enthralling mysteries.

Facebook @sabinawriter

Instagram @sabina.author

TikTok @sabina.author

ALSO BY

A Harry Sinclair Cozy Travel Mystery series so far:

Shadows of Serenity

Moonlit Secrets

Whispers of Lotus Villa (1st June 2025)

Sabina's Humorous Non-fiction Series:

The Crinkle Crankle Wall: Our First Year in Andalusia

A Hoopoe on the Nispero Tree: Our Andalusian Adventure Continues

Olive Leaf Tea: Time to Settle

ACKNOWLEDGEMENTS

Writing a book is never a solitary endeavor, and this cozy mystery, the first in the adventures of Harry Sinclair, is no exception. My journey from a budding idea to these pages has been accompanied by a remarkable group of individuals to whom I owe much gratitude.

First and foremost, my heartfelt thanks go to Denver Murphy, my editor. Denver, your experience and guidance in crafting a crime story has been instrumental in shaping this narrative. Your expertise brought Harry Sinclair's world to life with vivid detail and thrilling intrigue.

I am also immensely grateful to my beta readers and reviewers, whose insights were invaluable in refining this book. A special mention to Teri Kellum—not only for your detailed feedback but also for your family's advice on the technical aspects of CPR and crime scene details, which added authenticity and depth to the narrative. Linda Ann Foster and Mac Cochenour, your enthusiasm and encouragement throughout the reading of the beta version helped sustain my spirits and sharpen my focus.

To my fellow writers from the We Love Memoirs group—Val Poore, Dawne Archer, and Sue Bavey—thank you for your eagerness to dive into my new series and for providing honest, constructive reviews. Your support has been a source of motivation.

Last but certainly not least, my deepest appreciation to my husband, Robert Ryan. Robert, your support in reading through the various drafts have been nothing short of inspiring.

To all of you, my sincere thanks for your contributions, large and small, to this project. You have all left an indelible mark on this work, and I am profoundly thankful for each one of you.

PHOTO CREDITS

iStock photo credits:

Basil Chilli Squid iStock.com/Thai Liang Lim

Sushi iStock.com/alubalish

Mango Sticky Rice iStock.com/Kritchai Chaibangyang

Mai Tai iStock.com/bhofack2

Basil Mojito iStock.com/vasiliybudarin

Egg Omelet iStock.com/gkrphoto

Grilled Tiger Prawns iStock.com/Waqar Hussain

Pineapple Rice iStock.com/Supersmario

Coconut Cocktail iStock.com/Moncherie

Pad Kra Pao iStock.com/Andrei Kravtsov

Pixabay photo credits:

Grilled Sea Bass by GregReese

Breakfast Smoothies by phamkhanhquynhtrang

Fish Curry by joannawielgosz

Coconut Breeze Cocktail by sweetmellowchill

Printed in Great Britain
by Amazon

60509588R00122